ELSEWHERE

BOOKS BY TABITHA BAUMANDER

THE POWER AND THE BLOOD
ELSEWHERE

ELSEWHERE

TABITHA BAUMANDER

SPEAKING VOLUMES, LLC

NAPLES, FLORIDA

2011

ELSEWHERE

ISBN 978-1-61232-007-6

Library of Congress Control Number: 2010942881

CHAPTER 1

Heart pounding hard in her chest, Zoe Crane opened her bedroom door a crack and looked out. The second floor hall was dimly lit by the light coming through the half-closed bathroom door.

The bathroom was at the far end of the hall and the stairs began in the middle. Her parent's bedroom door, directly across from the top step, stood wide open.

Her parents lived in the self-contained world of religious fundamentalism. Parental authority was absolute, particularly when it came to daughters who tended to spend too much time with preoccupations like music that could lead to no decent end.

Tonight, for the first time in her life, Zoe was saying no to her parents. The sad thing was they wouldn't realize that she had done it until she failed to come downstairs for breakfast.

Even when they found her gone there was no way of knowing if they would understand. She hadn't thought the same way they had in so long she wasn't quite sure what they would think.

She would phone in the morning and try to explain. That is, if she ever managed to leave. It was strange, if you didn't look too closely, a simple act of bravery could look so much like cowardice. Was she declaring her independence or running away?

Zoe grabbed the straps of the pack on her back and crept forward. Beneath her feet, a loud wooden creak came from the protesting floor. Zoe's knees turned to rubber.

During the day it would have been hardly noticeable, a typical old house sound. Here and now, in the silence of the night, it howled like an old-time preacher bemoaning the fate an ungrateful child.

The faint sound of rustling blankets, accompanied by a deep-voiced muttering, came from the black hole across from the stairs. Zoe retreated into the privacy of her room.

The way her father slept, there was no exit. Sound asleep the man could hear a flea fart at fifty paces.

Feeling trapped, Zoe closed the door silently and surveyed her moonlit refuge. Usually kept "good girl" neat in the interests of pleasing her mother, it was now much more than that, it was spotless.

The place looked exactly like a picture in a magazine; the kind of magazine her mother read with an almost religious intensity. They were stuffed full of fat-free recipes and expert advice on how to raise your teenager daughter.

This room had been redecorated by her mother the previous fall. The door had been removed from her walk-in closet and shelves had been added so that it looked like a miniature library. The wall that had once held her bookshelves was covered with a system of wire baskets holding her neatly folded wardrobe.

Her old wooden desk had been repainted a tastefully textured tone to match the walls. It sat looking out the window, facing the back of the house. The top of the desk held only the computer, silently dreaming its electronic dreams, muffled in a clear plastic dust cover.

A large stuffed bear still handsome in spite of its advanced age sat on the same old bed. It was a relic of a trip to a fair on her fifth birthday. The old fellow stared into space as if remembering the days when life was simpler. A time when, yes mother and no mother, were all one needed to make life run smoothly.

The bed the bear sat on had been repainted but not replaced. The mattress was in poor condition and sagged noticeably. Zoe had been looking forward to something new but her father had definite ideas about the immediate future of all seventeen-year old girls.

In his mind they unfailingly got married and pregnant well before they turned twenty-four. If she was going to need a double bed sometime in the next five or six years, why buy a new single?

A sudden prolonged yowl came from somewhere just outside the bedroom window. Zoe's tightly strung nerves jumped. In response she gripped the straps of her backpack convulsively, as if trying to get a firm hold on this midnight view of her world. A wait for her father's footsteps brought no results.

If he had heard the strange echoing sound he must have simply rolled over and gone back to sleep. Nature had given her father a sensitive ear, but thankfully it had also given him the unique ability to fall asleep instantly.

Thanking fate for small favors, Zoe crossed to the window and peered out into the night. A bright round moon smiled down benignly on the stretch of nicely-fenced, carefully tended yards. The yards, in turn, belonged to old, well cared for brick homes. At this late hour those homes were all darkly and sensibly asleep.

The source of the midnight howl was very close. A small white cat sat on the flat roof of the kitchen, which stretched out immediately beneath her window. Its short downy fur reflected the moonlight as if it held a gentle power all its own.

The cat looked at Zoe, shifting its hindquarters impatiently. Its tail whipped through the air twice then wrapped itself around the front feet, tip twitching slightly. Gazing into the small yellow eyes Zoe read the message there and felt embarrassed. She had neglected something that was perfectly obvious.

Working almost silently Zoe pushed her desk out of the way and slid the window open. She then slipped her pack off her back, pushed it through the window and wiggled out herself. Standing on the kitchen roof and feeling the night air Zoe realized she also felt a thrill of the sort she hadn't had in a long time.

She was breaking the rules. She was breaking the rules in the middle of the night and going into forbidden territory. Looking up at the sky and greeting the stars from this different angle for the first time Zoe knew it was silly and childish to consider simply standing on the flat kitchen roof to be pushing boundaries but that's how it felt. A wide smile lighting her face Zoe closed the window then turned toward the small feline. This was just the beginning.

"Here I am, kitty," she whispered. "Any more good ideas?"

As if it understood, the cat's small pink tongue flicked out gave its nose a quick lick then the cat turned and walked slowly to the edge of the roof. After a quick look back, it catapulted into the darkness and was gone.

Opting for caution as opposed to speed, Zoe carefully dropped her bag over the edge of the flat roof then slid over herself; hanging on to the edge for one slow second before executing a rolling drop onto the thick soft grass below.

Once on her feet again she reclaimed her pack, and looked around for the cat. It was gone. Wishing it well and thanking it for its timely advice Zoe crept around the side of the house, reaching the quiet street without interruption.

A volcanic mixture of long pent-up feelings lent compulsive energy to Zoe's moving feet as she strode away from the house. She decided to take a walk and burn off some steam before heading for her intended destination. As she walked the vivid memory of a conversation that had taken place just that morning drifted through her mind.

"Zoe you really have to listen to me. You're never going to be anything close to what you want to be if you stay at home."

"Karen they mean well."

"I know that. I mean, God, my parents are both drunks if I could chose I'd pick yours in a minute. But what they're pushing you into is not what you need. Look, it won't be easy and you might not even make it, but if you never try you'll end up middle aged, up to your nose in kids and hating yourself for never stepping out and giving your dreams a chance."

She'd crossed her arms and eyed her best friend with her own version of her mother's "now tell me what you really mean" stare.

"I don't suppose the fact that you need help paying the rent has anything to do with all this?"

"Sure, I need a roommate. I don't want it to be just anyone though and I know you'll live up to your part of the deal. That doesn't change the fact that you have to get your parents to back off and give you space to breathe or get the hell out. Why you can go on defending them when they treat you like a prisoner or a robot I don't know."

4

Zoe smiled and took a deep breath of cool night air. Her parents were good people. She didn't hate them. She even found it hard to be angry with them. They honestly believed that when it came to their only child they knew what was best, and they had always got what they wanted, until now.

Up on the roof unseen by cat or girl a man shaped shadow appeared. Running up from the kitchen roof it looked as if the invisible figure of a man were walking past Zoe's bedroom window. Slowly listlessly it walked from one side of the kitchen to the other. It stood for a long minute as if waiting for Zoe to return. Gradually the shadow became soft, indistinct. In the end it drifted away like thick smoke on a listless breeze.

CHAPTER 2

She'd taken a half empty bus part of the way but for the most of the time Zoe had walked. She'd walked past nice houses with big lawns, past stores, past a movie theater where the staff were leaving for their beds. The friendly echoing goodnights floating her way on the evening breeze made the scene itself seem like something out of a film. The sort of scene where the hero is reminded how far removed he is from the everyday world.

The later it got the more the shadows seem to draw her eyes. She wasn't stupid. This was a big city and big cities could be dangerous. Tonight the shadows seemed populated by unseen eyes. They were eyes that waited for her to make the wrong move, eyes that seemed to say the wrong move had already been made.

It was now very late, later than Zoe ever remembered being awake, almost late enough to be early. She was walking down a narrow, poorly lit, city street lined with small houses. Not once since she had left home had anyone spoken to her, or questioned her purpose.

They were impersonal things these small stucco covered boxes she passed. They sat complacently on their minuscule big city lots dark window's watching her pass like empty eyes. They didn't know or care that she was walking among them, thinking, dreaming, trying not to feel so alone. It wasn't easy.

After an eternity in its shadows, the dark side street ended at a brightly lit commercial avenue. Zoe knew this place well, had walked along it with her mother many times. Without conscious choice of direction she simply continued on, grateful for the light.

If the lateness of the hour was intimidating on the dimly lit side street, the effect here was even stronger. The buses had stopped running, and even on this normally busy street the traffic had dwindled down to an intermittent trickle.

A taxi came toward her out of the distance and rumbled past echoing a silent rebuke.

"Go home. Don't run. Go home."

Message delivered, it left to whatever work it was fated to have that night. Zoe turned and watched it go. As the cab disappeared, a battered blue sports car pulled up beside her, slowing to walking speed. The driver beckoned her closer, smiling.

Revulsion filling her mouth with its acid taste, she gave this drive by shopper the finger. He laughed, returned the favor, and drove on.

Zoe swallowed and tried to shake the empty feeling that had hit her at the recognition of the man's business offer. It wasn't as if this was the first time this kind of misunderstanding had happened. This was a big city and she had been downtown at night before.

It was simply that tonight was different. Everything around her felt strangely new, the good things, and the bad. This time she was alone.

A shiver ran through her that was equal parts emotion and temperature. Zoe pulled the zipper of her spring jacket up as far as it would go. It was cool, cooler than she thought June temperatures usually got. Of course she'd never before been out at three in the morning.

"I am not running away. I am moving out."

The words slipped out without direction, a kind of verbal hick-up. Still, it was nice to hear it out loud, an audible counterpoint to her own inner monologue. Not very convincing, but nice.

"I am not running away!"

Even nicer, even louder, not loud enough for her feet to hear, they kept moving.

Her backpack was slung over one slumped shoulder. The bag and every-thing inside it had been bought with her own money. That fact was im-portant. It meant that she had to leave behind her treasured guitar, but it also meant they could not force her back by charging her with theft.

The idea that she had to allow for such behavior on her parent's part left a hollow ache in Zoe's stomach. This was a new feeling standing on your own; exciting and terrifying all at once. The lateness of the hour and the practical problem of what to do next didn't help matters either.

Suddenly, working during the day, and finishing high school at night didn't seem like such a good idea. Maybe she wasn't street-smart enough to be on her own. Maybe she ought to go back and try again.

"I AM NOT RUNNING AWAY!"

Closing her mouth with her hands, she stopped walking and looked around, hoping no one had heard the nerve-induced outburst. There was no one in sight and after a minute she relaxed.

Just ahead of her was a piece of darkness created by a pair of burned-out street lamps creating an almost tactile blot of darkness. In spite of that one exception this stretch of nighttime world was remarkably well lit. The things in the store windows, the cracks in the sidewalk, even the patterns of the curtains in the apartment windows above the stores stood out in a kind of surreal detail that defied belief.

The street was an old one. A long time ago it had been full of homes for the moneyed few. They had been big Victorian structures, some complete with small carriage houses for guests. Of course parallel to these few had been the army of servants that maintained that old privileged way of life.

It was a completely different world that was long gone. The houses that hadn't been torn down were either partitioned off into apartments or converted into offices. The spaces between these elegant relics were filled by stores with apartments on second and third floors.

The only other pedestrian, if he could be called that, was an old man sitting in a doorway. Zoe glanced across the street at him and immediately got the impression he was staring at some invisible thing that only he could see.

He didn't seem interested in the present, or the future. He had deep drowning eyes that held only the past. Curiously he reminded Zoe of the shadows she had passed to get to this place. He was just as visible and yet just as lacking in substance.

Mildly reassured, Zoe continued walking. This phantom wouldn't say a word if she screamed her fool head off. He was too busy with his own dead dreams. For a moment she wanted to cross the street and ask, "Old man, did your dreams die because you tried and failed, or did they die of simple neglect?"

The thought of asking made Zoe realize how very tired she was. The overpowering compulsive impulse that had kept her moving for almost three hours was swiftly beginning to play itself out. She should have knocked on Karen's basement apartment door three hours ago. Instead the desperate need to walk had brought her here.

In the distance, a park, no more than three blocks away, held promise. Perhaps it was time to find herself a bench. Just until morning. In the morning she would begin anew. It was too late to knock on anyone's door now.

Blinking her eyes against the sudden change in illumination Zoe stepped into the pool of darkness created by the two burned-out streetlights. In the middle of this dark blot, there was a tall ironwork gate closing off the lane between two buildings swung inward on silent hinges.

The movement slowed, then stilled Zoe's marching feet. It was dark down there, dark enough to hide a hundred reasons to run and a hundred more to be too afraid to move.

Zoe stared at the gate shifting gently on its hinges and a new and different feeling was born. It started with a heartbeat, then spread out to touch every inch of her body and mind. There was fear mixed up in this feeling, and awe, and wonder, and something else she thought she knew but could not name.

Zoe took a step toward the opening, so that she stood just outside the threshold. It didn't seem so dark down there now.

At the end of the passage there was a small sheltered moon lit yard with a tree, a bench and a tall wooden fence. A good place to spend the night.

"Oh I eat my beans with honey. I done it all my life."

Zoe spun around. The old man was on his feet near a street lamp, singing and looking at the sky. His clothes, once stylish in some distant past, hung off him as if the old threads were heavy with dirt. The dirt was so thick it blurred the color beneath so it looked as if he were clad in homespun dust.

"It makes the beans taste funny. But it keeps them on my knife."

His eyes turned away from the sky and fixed on her. They were empty. The past that had filled them was gone. Zoe wondered how he could use them to see with at all. They looked dead.

"The bells of hell go ting-a-ling-a-ling. For you and not for me."

The man took a step into the road, then another and another. He was standing on the center line now. Zoe could smell the strange sour odor of old wine and something more, something dead and dangerous.

She felt the emptiness of the street, the lateness of the hour. Trembling slightly she began to inch backward away from this frightening vision.

"For me the angel's sing-a-ling-a-ling. That's how it ought to be."

This time when he stopped singing he locked eyes with Zoe and smiled. Zoe felt a stab of soul searing terror and took a full step backward. As she did she crossed the threshold of the ironwork gate.

Her hand brushed the free swinging door. Startled by the sudden contact Zoe jumped and the gate began to move. Slowly it put a barred barrier between her and the strangely frightening figure in the center of the road. The noise of the door closing was soft, mundane. At the same time it felt like a defiant scream as if the mettle in the fence had once been armor worn to defend the helpless and the innocent.

At the sound of this clattering clink the dead-eyed man stopped as if splashed with cold water. Sorrow filled his face and his eyes were no longer empty. They were filled with the past.

He turned away from her and returned to his stoop. Sitting he leaned into the shadows, his old-man's mask of a face blending into the darkness like a forgotten dream.

CHAPTER 3

Zoe backed away from the mouth of the narrow alley. Fear made her heart do hick-ups. Her fingers were icy cold and her face felt flushed and hot.

The old man had slumped into the shadows of his doorway with only his battered shoes topped off by ragged pants remaining bathed in the light of the street. Zoe felt his unseen eyes, glowing and alive in the wind-blown desert that was his face.

Should she sneak out now and make a run for it, or should she continue through the darkness to the secluded yard? Staying here was risky. There was no way of knowing, from where she stood, if there was another way out of the garden. Going down to investigate this potential resting place could be a good way to get trapped.

Making a run for it was the smart thing to do. It made sense. Only she didn't want to go anywhere else. There was a rightness about being here, a belonging, a feeling that this was what she'd been looking for all along.

Reluctantly Zoe took a step out toward the street, thinking to check on what the old man was doing. She reached out and gripped one of the bars of the gate. It felt warm and, frightened as she was, Zoe still had the presence of mind to wonder why?

Zoe stepped up to the gate and looked through. The old man was no-where to be seen. He had either pulled his legs completely into the darkness of the doorway or he had moved off. With his going the street itself had changed. The detail that had ingrained itself upon her eye and mind had melted into the shadows.

The whole avenue had a strange blurry look. The colors had lost their definition, blending into a sepia-tone haze. It the space of less than a minute it had become a different world.

Zoe lay a hand on the latch, thinking to step out and make sure he had gone. Suddenly distracted, she stopped and stared at her hand. It was trembling, registering its discomfort with what she proposed to do.

More than that, her whole body was radiating a silent message. No. Don't go back. You've come this far. You know you want to go down there. There's something about this place that's pulling you. Go and look. You will never have this chance again!

It was wrong and right all at once. Wrong in that it probably wasn't safe. Right in the simple fact that she had been so frighteningly predictable her whole life, something had to break.

"Father, I don't see what you have against my doing this. It's not going to interrupt with my regular studies. I know I need a day job to go along with the music."

"It's not proper for you to be associating with those people."

This explosion had begun years ago with a crack. That crack came in the form of a simple awareness when she entered her teens that the people around her had at least some say about what went on in their world. They chose their own clothes, clubs, hair styles, any number of things over which her own parents had always held strict control.

"What if I think it is proper?"

It had ended tonight with the last of a yearlong series of battles over what she would do with the rest of her life.

"I'm your father. I'll tell you what's proper and what isn't!"

"If you will excuse me, Father, I think I'm tired. I'm going to bed."

With that last quiet statement she had declared an end to all fights and disagreements. She was in charge now. It wasn't a very comfortable feeling. Thinking, planning, even dreaming about the future was something you had to practice. She had never been given the chance to do so out in the open and secret daydreams weren't the same.

Zoe turned away from the gate. Maybe it was time to practice dreaming out in the open. No. Maybes didn't belong in here behind this gate. In fact, dreaming had never been easier. The ground in this narrow space was paved with the same dark red brick used in the buildings.

The walls on either side were without windows. The whole corridor looked as if a wide cobblestone road. It was a road that had been bent by some force pushing toward the speed of light in a desperate attempt to leap past reality.

Holding her bag to her chest, Zoe fixed her eyes on the sheltered arbor ahead of her and began to walk. She felt dizzy, as if she were walking a thin plank two hundred feet in the air. The walls were no help. Suddenly she couldn't tell just where they were, they could be close enough to touch, or they could be a thousand-miles away. Only the thing that had brought her here could save her from falling, from slipping into fear.

On the other side of the gate it had no name. In here it did. In here that thing was called desire. It labeled all the petty, mundane rules of life irrelevant and set them aside. All time but now had gone.

Zoe stepped out of the brickwork canyon and into the moonlit arbor. It was a grassy space enclosed by a tall wooden fence with no gate. Flowering vines clung too much of this fence giving the space the illusion of a wooded glen. Hugging the edges were rose bushes and several other flowering shrubs. A long wooden bench under a massive old willow tree was placed to the left of center while an actual operating fountain took up much of the right.

The effect was awe inspiring. It was a plot of land where a person with a practical turn of mind would have found a hard time parking more than three cars. To Zoe - standing in the only entrance - it looked like a small slice of Eden. One, two, three, four steps across the thick springy grass brought her to the bench.

Sitting brought a hollow ache from her feet. The feeling traveled up her legs and made her tired mind scream for sleep. The bag was too bulky to be pressed into service as a pillow, so she pulled a sweatshirt from its depths, balled it up and lay down. Almost immediately the dream space around her began to blur. The swimming, floating feeling of rest long denied began to take charge of her world.

"Are you quite comfortable?"

A dream... just a dream.

"I only ask because it is rather cool. In an hour or two the dew will begin to settle and that will make you somewhat damp."

Not a dream, a voice from above.

"You're free to stay there, or come up and use my couch. It's long and soft and has a warm quilt. I tend to doze off on it myself."

A woman's voice. A woman's shape, silhouetted by the moon, made indistinct by the interwoven branches of the willow. The shape stood on the uppermost platform of the fire escape gracing the rear of the building to the right of the lane.

Puzzled by this strangely civil reception in the face of blatant trespass, Zoe stood and stepped out from under the sheltering branches of the tree. The woman's face was impossible to see properly from this angle. Her age was difficult to tell.

"I've put the kettle on. We'll have tea, then I'll let you get some sleep."

The woman began to go through the door she stood in front of, then turned back. Zoe knew that move. It was a mother's gesture impatient but not unkind.

"Come along, girl. I won't ask a second time. You have a mind. Use it."

Leaving her things behind, Zoe climbed the metal steps. Her feet made echoing tap, tap, sounds. In its turn, the ironwork scaffolding she climbed made barely audible creeks, as if unwilling to interrupt the natural quiet of this pocket paradise. The only other sound was the gentle splashing trickle of water from the fountain.

Tired as she was Zoe wondered what sort of woman invited trespassers in for a comfortable nap? She wondered, but she no longer had the strength to do much more. A hollow emptiness resounded in her breast. Echoes and images of home flashed through her mind. They were memories of the same old bed and the same old comforting routine. It was a routine, which in truth had not been comfortable in a long time.

She would take a look, just a look, and if she didn't like what she saw, she would go.

CHAPTER 4

Zoe crested the final step on the fire escape and stood for a moment on the top landing looking out at the world from this second floor perch. From here she could see back-gardens, houses, and beyond them streets. Nowhere was there a bit of space as beautiful as the one she had just left, and nowhere did a light shine to show that anyone was awake.

Zoe turned to find the back door to the apartment was open. The woman stood looking through the screen door, waiting. A moment of silent assessment passed between them.

"I've been expecting you. My name is Yolanda Wren."

Zoe's tired mind spun with the impossibility of the woman's statement. How could you expect someone who didn't know they were coming? She tried to ask but all she could manage to say was;

"Hi, I'm Zoe Crane."

"Welcome Zoe Crane. Enter of your own free will. Right foot forward if you please."

Yolanda Wren opened the door, standing aside to allow Zoe to enter. Zoe stepped toward the door then stopped. Confused she looked from the door to the woman.

"I'm, not sure what you mean," she said.

"Step in with your right foot first. It's an old custom. Older than many people realize."

Understanding now Zoe entered the room as instructed. Yolanda Wren let the screen door swing shut with a quiet clump.

"You look tired. Sit. I'll make the tea."

They were in a kitchen, with a table and chairs set against the building's rear wall. The sink, with a small work space on either side, was opposite. Across from the exit, a closed door separated the kitchen from the rest of the apartment. Zoe did as instructed, choosing a chair between the table and the exit.

The state the room was in hovered somewhere between what Zoe considered casually clean, and something close to complete disaster. It gave the impression that whoever lived here, although not deliberately lazy, generally had better things to do than wipe counters.

In contrast to the rest of the room, the table was immaculate. On it sat a china tea pot with a lustrous blue finish that glowed with a life of its own. Next to the pot sat two matching mugs, two tea bags and a deck of tarot cards.

The pottery, obviously not mass-produced, interested Zoe, but the cards drew her attention and held it like a magnet. She knew what they were, but never had she seen a deck that showed such clear signs of constant use. On the back of the topmost card and presumably on each one underneath was the picture of a small white cat.

The woman who had called herself Yolanda Wren made an even bigger impression than her kitchen. Her short tousled hair was almost completely gray. What hair that was not gray was a light chestnut brown.

She had a medium build and wore a long flowing peasant blouse over loose cut jeans. Both items had seen better days and yet they seemed almost a part of her, a segment of her personality without which she would be diminished in some indescribable way.

Her age was a mystery. Her emerald green eyes held a fire Zoe had never seen before. In the world Zoe had left behind she might have been thought an old woman. But old woman's eyes did not glow like this.

"I hope you like chamomile. I find it particularly appropriate for this time of night. Three AM is the time when the soul is laid bare and pretense fades away. We who are awake to face this process need all the help we can get."

Her voice was deep and soothing like a warm blanket or a well-kept secret. As she spoke she carried a steaming copper kettle from the stove to the table where she poured water into the teapot and dropped in the bags. After the top to the pot was replaced she returned the kettle to the stove then came and sat opposite her guest.

To Zoe these commonplace movements were almost hypnotic in their simplicity. Every mundane act held a hundred different meanings, each

16

meaning in turn holding a thousand different scraps of knowledge. Knowledge was power and some inner part of Zoe's mind knew that this was what this woman had, and what she needed.

"I'll be Mother, shall I?"

Zoe only nodded. In response Yolanda Wren lifted the pot and poured out two mugs full of steaming yellowish liquid. Zoe took the mug closest to her, finding a curious strength in the simple act of holding the warm object and breathing in its perfume.

"How could you be expecting me?" Zoe asked finally.

Yolanda held up the cards.

"By using these."

"They're tarot cards right?"

"Yes, that's right. I'm very good. That sounds egotistical I know, but it is the truth. I've made a living doing it for more years than you've been alive and on nights like this I am never wrong. You need my help."

Zoe knew the woman was right, but before she could let the budding free spirit inside her speak, another voice interrupted. The voice was hers, but her father lived in the tone, the word choice, the essential, careful, ordinariness of it all. Her mother was there too, quietly insisting that common sense and good manners prevail.

"This isn't what it looks like. I have three-thousand dollars in the bank, and a friend who has been after me to move in with her. The office where I work part-time at night needs some full-time help during the day."

"A place to go and money to take you there," Yolanda observed. "Yet you sneak about like a thief in the night. Do you know why?"

Zoe held her mug close, letting its heat support her sagging will. Honesty was hard, but it was the only thing those fiery green eyes were going to accept. It was also quite likely the only thing that would keep her from slipping back though her bedroom window and going on as if none of this had ever happened.

"I feel like I'm running away. There's an empty spot where my self-confidence should be. I'm afraid."

"How did you happen to be in my garden?"

17

Zoe thought back and found a strange blur had slipped into the part of her memory holding the time between this place and home. On the other side of the table Yolanda Wren waited patiently, as if she knew the answer might be a long time in coming.

"I don't know. I feel like I've been walking forever. Right now I'm not even sure I remember where. I do know for the first little while I couldn't stop walking, then I didn't want to. I think I rode a bus for a time. There were crowds, then the crowds thinned out. It got late, too late to call my friend."

"I don't think you wanted to," said Yolanda. "You're a sensitive person, an intuitive person. You may not realize it, but you are. Life is handing you a conservative script and without understanding why, you know you belong elsewhere, if only for a time."

Zoe took a sip of the tea. It had a strange taste, harsh and at the same time a little sweet. Across the table Yolanda Wren also sipped her tea. She smiled a small enigmatic smile, the sort of smile artists went mad trying to capture.

In the light of that smile Zoe realized she did know at least part of what she wanted to learn. It was a small part of what had pushed her out her bedroom window. There was a lot more naturally but all the rest depended on this one thing.

"I think I want the chance to make up my own mind. The problem is I'm not sure if I know how."

Zoe followed this revelation with a long drink. Freedom of expression was a strange and confusing thing. At home with her mother this conversation would have taken the form of freeze-dried opinion and carefully learned response. Here in this small dimly lit kitchen it felt like the limits of the cosmos itself were only mildly irritating distractions, easily gotten around if necessary.

"You need to go elsewhere," said Yolanda Wren. "And if you're walking, this is as close to elsewhere as one can get."

"I don't understand."

Zoe looked across the table at her hostess and saw that Yolanda Wren's disarming smile had vanished. In its place came a look that Zoe did not understand, a look of dispassionate judgment.

"Not many find my garden, Zoe Crane. Even fewer enter. Why did you enter my garden?"

"It would have been wrong not to," answered Zoe.

The words slipped out without direction, asserting the truth as all good words should.

"Promising. This shows you're listening. A promising truth indeed."

Yolanda's smile reappeared like a flash of sun and was gone just as quickly. Zoe relaxed a little. Honesty had dividends.

"What am I listening to?" Zoe asked.

"If you knew that you wouldn't need to be here."

A gem of frustration started in the back of Zoe's mind.

"What is this, some kind of word game?"

Yolanda shook her head firmly.

"No. It's the truth. The truth is not a game. Drink your tea. I will look at your cards and then you must sleep."

The smile returned. It was reassuring, and yet with the energy it held, a little unsettling. Yolanda took a sip of her tea and set the mug aside. She took the tarot deck, removed the elastic band that held it together then put the band beside her mug.

"Shuffle, then cut the cards into three piles."

The cards were bigger than normal playing cards. It was a struggle to do as she was asked without dropping them all over the floor but Zoe managed to do as she was asked.

"Which part shall I read?" Yolanda asked.

After an uncertain moment Zoe tapped the center pile of cards.

"That one."

Yolanda gathered up the other two and set them aside. After collecting the final pile she turned the cards over, one by one, laying them out face up in rows of four. The woman looked at the strange pictures in front of her for a long time, then leaned back in her chair, returning her attention to her guest.

"I was right. You belong elsewhere. You see, to grow up whole, one must have a personal knowledge, or at least an awareness, of many things. If a person realizes they will never get what they need where they are, a change takes place. Hopefully for the better, but not always. Your change has begun tonight."

"Why was I supposed to come here? What do I need here that I can't get out there?"

Zoe turned from Yolanda to the open kitchen door. The garden felt a long way away. Her home, her home was light years distant.

"What do you need? You need adventure, passion, danger; you need to learn how strong you are. These things are out there in plentiful supply, but not for you, or you would not have come here. Because you took the first step, the rest of your journey was almost a forgone conclusion. Your walk is over. You are where you need to be."

CHAPTER 5

Zoe felt lost. This woman seemed to understand what she was feeling, her need to get away, and her desire to stand on her own. Why she felt the need to surround her understanding with the language of poetry and fantasy was a question for which Zoe had no answer.

The only thing Zoe understood about this entire unorthodox interview was that she had found a safe haven. For now that was enough. She placed her mug on the table, rose and closed the kitchen door, shutting out the night.

"If you don't mind, I think I'd like to try out that couch now."

"Follow me."

The door opposite the exit opened into a dark narrow hall running the length of the building. On the right a steep set of stairs led down to a door facing the street. On the left there were three doors, two of them open. At the end of the hall there was another open door showing a room facing the street. Light shining through a window showed that this distant place was the living room, the refuge where she would finally get some sleep.

The first open door they passed revealed the bathroom. A small light above the medicine chest gave Zoe a glimpse of a claw footed tub, a pedestal sink, and a toilet that might have begun its service shortly after the First World War.

The next room, lit by a small reading lamp, was a bedroom. A large display cabinet set across from the door was bursting with what looked like antique toys. This strange eclectic mix of treasures caught Zoe's attention, stilling her moving feet. Seeing Zoe's interest Yolanda stopped as well.

"It's my collection. A cabinet full of dreams and adventure."

"Why does the glass look so strange?"

Yolanda shrugged slightly.

"It isn't glass. It's plastic wrap. It keeps out the dust. I had an accident when I was about your age. I fell into the glass and the whole thing shattered. I was lucky. Not only did I not destroy the cabinet, I didn't even get cut. I've never had the money to replace the glass. Come to think of it, maybe

I've simply never wanted to, I don't know. What happened once could happen again."

Again the almost luminous smile lit Yolanda Wren's face. She continued to the end room, bypassing the third door. Zoe followed slipping off her coat as she went. Stopping at the living room entrance she turned back.

"What's that room?"

This time ignoring Zoe's interest Yolanda flicked on the living room light and went to the couch where she began spreading out a thick quilt. For the first time her voice was matter of fact, with a kind of disinterested pragmatism.

"That's my client room," she said.

"Client room?" asked Zoe.

"If anyone else lived here, it would probably be used as another bedroom. It's where I give readings. They drink their tea in here and then we go in there and I read tea leaves, cards, and crystal."

Yolanda came back to the entrance of the living room.

"Go ahead, look. I'm not hiding anything. I have nothing to hide. The light switch is to the left of the door. There's nothing much in there. It's a small room with a table, two chairs and a closet. I find the simplicity helps my concentration."

Wondering why she was suddenly apprehensive Zoe went to the door, opened it and turned on the ceiling light. The walls were painted a deep blue. In the center of the small room there stood a round wooden table with two chairs, one on either side. In the center of the table was a shiny crystal sphere.

The sight of the ball drew Zoe to the table where she sat in one of the chairs. Yolanda Wren appeared in the doorway.

"My crystal ball. It was given to me by an old woman who, in turn, got it from her grandmother. That woman got it from some other elder. I was never told who. When things like this are very old, they take on a life of their own."

Zoe nodded only half hearing. Yolanda frowned slightly at this hypnotic preoccupation.

"The process is called scrying. Once you know what you're doing you can see the future, the past, any number of things. Sometimes people see their past lives. Sometimes they see something else entirely."

Zoe did not notice when Yolanda Wren left her alone. She only noticed the light. This ball, this strange half cloudy sphere, held an oddly powerful light.

The longer she sat staring into the depths of the sphere the brighter the light grew. It called to her. Its beams penetrated into the empty places in her heart and mind and offered an unspoken answer. Slowly her hand reached up and out to touch the ball.

*****

Yolanda Wren entered her living room brow lined in confusion. She was taking a pillow from a cedar trunk end-table when the pre-dawn silence was broken by a high pitched whine.

Yolanda grabbed her ears against the wild sound. Long, loud, piercing; it ending with a muffled thump like a hand hitting the cover of a very thick, very old book. Stunned by the auditory attack that had brought her to her knees, Yolanda Wren pulled herself onto the sofa with trembling hands, staring all the while in the direction of the door.

A slight tremor in her voice she called, "Zoe? Zoe Crane? Are you all right?"

After a long moment, she stood and returned to the other room taking a large square of black velvet out of a pants pocket. Looking strictly at the floor she entered the room carrying the cloth ahead of her like a shield. Only after the square of cloth covered the ball in the center of the table did Yolanda Wren look up. Zoe was gone.

"Good Goddess, why didn't I see this happening?"

Other than a single tipped-over chair and Zoe's jacket, there were no physical signs that anything had happened. Hands trembling slightly, Yolanda picked up the ball and finished wrapping it in the cloth taking care not to look at or touch the smooth glassy surface.

23

Carrying it gently in cupped hands she took it to her bedroom. Mixed up with the toys in the cabinet standing in her bedroom was another, slightly smaller, ball, resting on a small wooden ring. Next to it was a silver ring, elaborately engraved.

Yolanda placed the wrapped up ball on this ring and removed the smaller ball complete with its stand. This she returned to the small bare room, placing it in the center of the round table. Returning to the living room she turned off the light. The room was bathed again in the distant glow of the street lamps.

Yolanda turned to leave the room, then stopped as if disturbed by some far off, half-heard sound. She moved, following the sound to the window and looked out.

"Shadow man."

He stood by a street lamp, dressed in dust-gray rags, arms hanging limp at his sides, eyes looking straight into her soul. He had been before she existed. He would be when she was long gone. She was the keeper of the crystal and he existed like a shadow cast by the crystals light.

"Shadow Man, Shadow Man, eater of dreams. You have no more business here. The traveler has gone."

She spoke the words in a whisper. A whisper she knew he could hear.

"Witch Woman, Witch Woman, I know more than most when I have failed. But you have failed as well. This little one has traveled alone without preparation or aid. Name me the odds against her return!"

His sour laugh burned itself into her mind like an acid. Unable to escape its power, Yolanda fell onto the couch and buried her face in the pillow she had laid out for Zoe Crane. Finally, mercifully, the laughter subsided and when she looked again, the Shadow Man was gone.

Dressed for bed some minutes later Yolanda Wren looked at the cloth wrapped ball on its stand. The velvet shifted, rising slightly as if moved by some inner energy, then subsiding. Yolanda Wren nodded almost imperceptibly.

"That's normal enough. We'll have to see, I suppose. It's not as if I haven't spent time waiting before."

24

There was confusion in her eyes, a helpless resignation in the set of her shoulders. She turned away from the cabinet.

As she did this, her eyes rested on Zoe's back pack which she had retrieved from the garden. It sat leaning against the end of her bed like a faithful dog waiting for its master's return.

Sighing deeply, Yolanda Wren crawled into bed, turned out the light and went to sleep.

CHAPTER 6

The small blue room was gone. In its place came a rushing of wind followed by an absence of all physical sensation. Light was dots of distant fire cutting through the blackness. One light, surrounded by a multicolored halo of energy, flashed in a regular beat. It pulled and she followed. As she drew toward it the light grew blinding, then dimmed. Then everything went completely black.

A cluster of sensations pulled Zoe out of the blackness, giving her a sense of place. The first was tar paper embedded with a thin layer of small stones which pebbled themselves into her cheek and hands. The smell of a lake perfumed by one too many factories assaulted her nose in the same way the gravel scratched at her skin. A listless breeze did its best to move the still, warm, air.

Words echoed in Zoe's mind.

"If you're walking, this is as close to elsewhere as you can get."

A prophetic sounding statement, understood less now than before.

Zoe took a deep breath. The result was marginally successful. It only hurt a little.

Breathing was the only thing that hurt a little. Everything else hurt a lot. The only comparison Zoe could think of was one with which she had no personal experience.

Drinking had never been one of her interests. But she had heard from friends, in graphic detail, about being badly hung-over. If one compared the symptoms they had described to whatever this was, Zoe guessed that she would have preferred the hang-over. At least a hangover had the benefit of being preceded by a party.

"Beware of strange women bearing crystal balls."

Zoe winced against the sudden pain speaking had brought, then swallowed, resolving not to talk again until her throat showed some sign of recovery.

The first objects that came into view when she opened her eyes were an old fashioned valise and a battered guitar case. They weren't hers. The valise did look very much like the old over-night case she'd had as a child, but that had fallen apart years ago. The guitar, well, maybe her guitar case did look like this one, but most of those things tended to look alike. Didn't they?

It couldn't have been hers. She hadn't even looked at her guitar in almost a month. Heartily tired of listening to her father compare the amount of time she played the instrument to the amount of time she spent doing homework, she had set the instrument aside in protest. That protest been completely misunderstood, leaving her father triumphant again.

Moving with slow motion gentleness, Zoe rolled onto one side and pushed up into something close to a sitting position. The inside of her head did pirouettes in protest and her vision swam, momentarily producing enough suitcases and guitars to equip a dozen musical travelers.

Zoe had an idea that if she could just get her body moving this strange sickness would pass. All she had to do, was do it, but doing it was not going to be easy.

Now that Zoe was sitting up she could see where she lay. She was on the roof of what looked like an old factory or warehouse. The light she saw by came from nearby street lamps. The wide flat roof was dotted with ventilation chimneys and rimmed by a waist-high brick fascia. Running along the center of the building were two large skylights. On the other side of the building stood a small brick booth. A door hung on one rusty hinge. Hopefully this offered a way down.

Closer to where she sat, the top of a fire-escape gave her a choice of exit. What about her entrance? The memory of how she had arrived here to begin with was shrouded in a fog. Laid over the mist like a projection was the clear image of an impossible dream.

Backing away from the dream Zoe tried to attack the problem by steps. The beginning was the moment she had entered the small blue room. Gripped by a pull she still didn't understand she had sat. Her hand had reached out to touch the ball. A light had been in it, a strange, bright light, pulling, inviting. After the touch had come the dream.

It had been a wonderful dream, more vivid than any she had ever had. Could it have been some sort of hallucination? Could looking in the crystal ball have triggered something in her mind? Perhaps something strange had been painted on the ball. A hallucinogenic drug absorbed through the skin could be capable of turning true memory into some sort of symbolic dream.

She'd read that people on drugs often forgot large chunks of time. Forgotten time. Easy words to read, a hard truth to swallow.

Looking over at the valise she wondered if she had been alone the whole time, and was she still alone? Where was the owner of this strangely familiar luggage? Where was she?

As Zoe pondered these questions the eastern horizon grew gray, then the gray became touched with blue. Feeling stronger now, she stood and looked beyond the boundaries of her quiet sanctuary. The result caused her spirits to dip drastically.

This was definitely not Toronto. The building she stood on was between the waterfront and the city's downtown. There were no-glass covered skyscrapers, no soaring waterfront communications tower. In fact, there were no familiar land marks at all. Instead, the tableau gave the impression of huge amounts of stone, brick and cement.

It looked as if this city's whole downtown had been built by the same man who had built the Empire State Building. This was some other city. As sickening as the thought was, it was clear that she must have lost days, perhaps even weeks!

It had been cool. Now even at this early hour it was warm, almost hot.

She had been in a mixed residential-commercial area of Toronto, Canada. Now she was on a roof of some city on a lake. It might not even be the same lake. What city in North America had kept its urban area looking like some kind of 1920s' post card?

Now that dawn was taking control of the countryside, many odd things stood out for questioning. A passenger train passed between the building and the water on an elevated track. The sight triggered distant memories of old black and white movies watched on lonely weekend afternoons. The engine, the passenger cars, the whole train was the type seldom seen outside amusement parks and museums.

Looking down into the street gave Zoe another puzzle to add to her growing list. A large, black, vintage limousine sat next to the curb. Like the train, it too was museum quality. Two more cars drove along the barren street, then a taxi. All three were vintage models, not as nice as the limousine, but in good condition.

The really confusing part was the taxi. As it drove off into the distance Zoe could see quite clearly through the back window. It had a passenger.

That didn't make sense. Why would anyone owning a vintage car turn it into a working taxi? If it wasn't an actual working taxi why were the people inside sitting one in front, one in back?

Three muffled explosions, the first two accompanied by shower of glass, caused Zoe to look behind her in time to see the last of the glass fall to the roof in a tinkling spray. One of the eight windowed skylights now had three glass panes shattered. The silence that followed was broken by two men's voices, coming from inside the building. One was filled with a strangely impotent rage, the other might have been playing chess.

"I'm going to get you for that, you bastard, if I have to come back from hell to do it!"

Kendel, for someone to come back from somewhere, they first have to go. This is something you are going to be doing, very, very soon."

CHAPTER 7

Joshua Kendel watched the life go out of his assistant's eyes. A pool of red was spreading out from underneath the body.

The man had worked with an informant for six months. The stool pigeon had enabled them to arrest several small players in this grim game of crime but tonight he had promised information that would get the big man himself, Nick Tolino. He would deliver that is if the head district attorney would come to the meeting himself. It had all been a trap.

They'd been overpowered, battered, bound and then thrown into the trunk of a car to be delivered here. Tolino had then arrived to deliver an ultimatum. Lay off or die. His assistant had told the man to go to hell. Now he was dead.

Tolino took his time putting the still smoking gun back into his shoulder holster. He then crossed in front of Kendel. Kendel stiffened, trying to ready himself for whatever might come next.

A fist like cement went into his mid-section twice and all the strength went out of his legs. He slumped in the arms of the two men who held him. Then they let him fall. Looking up at the broken skylight Kendel saw the morning light and knew this day would be his last.

*****

Zoe approached the broken window on legs trembling with fear. Avoiding the glass as much as possible she knelt and peeked in through the shattered opening. Within was a dim industrial cavern lit only by the sky light and a single hanging bulb.

One man lay on the floor directly beneath the window. He was dressed in a plain white shirt and gray trousers. His hands were bound behind his back.

The dark red stain spreading out from beneath him had a matching blotch directly over his heart. Another man, his hands also bound behind him, lay in a crumpled heap as if he had just received a heavy blow.

As frightening as this unexpected sight was, what Zoe could see of the figures who stood in a rough circle around the dead man and his friend gave the scene had an overpowering aura of lurid unreality. There were eight of them, each resplendent in a pin-striped suit with wide lapels and a gray or brown fedora hat. If it weren't for the bullets, which had broken the windows, she would have assumed they were rehearsing for a play.

One man, standing just inside the curiously tailored circle, had lost his hat. A member of the circle picked it up and brushed it off before handing it over. It was difficult to tell from overhead, but the man who took the hat seemed better dressed than the rest.

Well-dressed or not, he was obviously in charge. When he spoke it was with a voice that had seen the inside of far too many smoke-filled rooms.

"Remind me. Did old man Morrelli pay his protection this week?"

A stout man, more muscle than fat, but with both in plentiful supply, took a notebook out of an inner pocket and consulted it. As he did this he exuded a fastidious kind of efficiency that turned Zoe's stomach. If this strange scene wasn't some kind of play, a man was dead, and this over-muscled bookkeeper was standing there calmly consulting his ledger!

"He paid half," the man announced finally.

"Half? He paid half and you let him get away with it?"

"He had a good reason, Boss. Business was bad this week. His foreman died. Morrelli said he drank some bad booze. Most of the staff went to the wake and now three of them are in the hospital for the same reason."

"Our stuff?"

"Yeah."

"We gotta get a better mix. We're killing off business."

The Boss wandered the floor, first out of Zoe's line of sight then across it again. As he returned he stepped carefully around the growing pool of blood. It was as if the dead man lying there were nothing more than a mess to be avoided.

He stopped in front of a large machine. It consisted of four large sections each one connected by a long bed of rollers. To Zoe, who could only see part of it, it looked like a thing constructed to make a great deal of noise while performing a simple task in the most awkward way possible.

"What is this thing?" asked the boss.

The bookkeeper, moved to his boss's side.

"It washes carpets. It's just like how my wife does shirts, only all automatic. Wash tub down one end, then a rinse tub, then a ringer to get most of the water out, then a press to iron the thing dry. All they have to do, is hook the rug up to one of those bars and the machine does the rest."

The boss studied his minion with pointed curiosity.

"How do you know all this stuff?"

"I take an interest in our clients' needs," answered the bookkeeper. "Also, I figure someday, if I live long enough to retire, I'll want something to do."

The boss laughed at this comment, clearly meant more as a joke than as some serious ambition. He pointed to the still living man on the floor.

"All right let's give you a chance to practice. Bring him over here."

Two of the hoods picked up the intended victim and dragged him across the cement. The movement seemed to revive the man and he began to take an interest in what was happening.

By the time they got to the carpet washer he was standing under his own power. The little group stood beside the platform located between the wide wringer rollers that squeezed the excess water out of the carpets and the huge press, which finished the drying process. The press consisted mainly of a massive iron plate fixed to a piston. This space was cluttered with a large number of bars with clamps attached to chains.

"Tie his feet to one of the bars and turn it on," ordered the Boss.

"Which one?" asked one of the men.

"Pick one, Stupid," said the bookkeeper. "The machine pulls them through one at a time. Sooner or later it'll get to him. You don't mind waiting a few extra minutes do you, Mister Kendel?"

"Just take care of it," said the Boss. "I'll be in the car."

The head man and two larger shadows left. One of the remaining men held the battered Kendel, while a second disappeared into the shadows, then reappeared with two lengths of thick cord.

They then lifted him onto the bed of rollers that lay between the huge wringers and the press. When the two men stepped away from the machine Zoe could see their victim was limp and breathing heavily, as if he had expended much of his remaining energy fighting against their iron grip.

When she looked for his feet, they were hard to see. The men had attached him to the bottom-most rod on the machine. He would have to lie there for some time, helpless, watching the killer piston move up and down before he was finally pulled under.

"Why do you play toad to that creep, Malone?"

Kendel's voice was faint and breathless.

"You could do a lot better on your own."

The man Zoe now knew as Malone seemed annoyed by this comment.

"Shut up, Kendel! Unless, of course, you'd rather go through the entire wash cycle before you get flattened. Y'know, I kind of admire your guts. But somehow I think getting half-drowned twice, then dragged between hot rollers will take the starch out of even you."

"I'd be just as dead."

Kendel's voice was flat and empty, as if he knew his time was almost finished.

"Ah, but as my sainted mother once said to me: 'It isn't being dead that frightens people, my boy it's dying. Once you're dead, it's over and you're in heaven.' But getting to the 'it's over' part can be hell on earth."

Laughing, Malone stepped away from the man on the machine. The two remaining musclemen looked at him questioningly. He cocked his thumb in the direction the Boss and their compatriots had gone. They took the hint and left.

When the musclemen had gone, Kendel asked, "How did such a smart mother beget such a stupid son?"

Malone stopped laughing. His voice sounded hard and humorless.

"I have a better question for you."

He walked to the wall and grasped the handle of a large H-shaped switch. "How did such a smart man end up dying in such a stupid way?"

Malone moved the switch so that the handle pointed skyward. He left without looking back.

Somewhere inside the machine, an engine began to hum.

CHAPTER 8

Zoe raced for the door into the building the second Malone was out of her line of sight. She had only two fears as she ran. The first involved not getting to this Kendel in time and listening to him scream as he was pulled under the hot piston to his death.

The second was more complex and, she had to admit to herself, a bit more selfish. She had no guarantee that the strange men with their gangster-movie outfits would not come walking out of the dark shadows. If she was caught dragging their victim off his murderous bed she would earn herself a death sentence. She might die without ever learning where she was!

Squeezing past the broken door, Zoe stepped down a handful of metal stairs onto a catwalk world made of iron struts and pipes bolted to the ceiling. Below her lay a dark open space filled with machinery.

Some of this industrial collection was orderly, as if the big machines were used regularly. The rest was an eclectic mix of sprawling things. They were ominous objects that cast macabre shadows and smelled of motor oil and dirt.

For some reason the building had been hung with a system of cat walks reaching to every part of the structure. It quickly became very clear, however, that the system belonged to one of the building's former tenants; possibly the same one that had used the neglected machinery.

On one end a chain blocked off the space where a ladder or stairs had once been. Zoe slid to a halt.

"Damn! You're a lot of use aren't you? Now where?"

She turned and looked down the length of the walk she had gone along. At the far end she saw what looked like the beginning of another stairway, this set of stairs was not blocked by a chain!

"Yes! We have a winner! No chain means there must be stairs."

Zoe ran run full speed toward this avenue of hope. When she arrived, however, she learned that on this end the building's owners had not been quite as considerate as they had on the opposite end.

Here the beginning of a set of spiraling stairs led straight into dark nothingness! Zoe grabbed the railing and clung, peddling her feet in mid-air. Kicking her legs toward the catwalk she found the strength to get her legs hooked on the metal. Slowly she pulled herself back up rolling onto the platform.

"Some hero. I almost got myself killed before the victim."

Gasping for breath she peered into the gloom. Now her eyes had fully adjusted to the sparse illumination she could see quite clearly that two other ladders had once existed on the other side of the building. Unfortunately they had also been dismantled. There was no way down!

On the factory floor the motor of the huge rug washer had warmed up and an echoing hissing thud announced the fact that the massive iron had begun to press its non-existent product. Not sure what to do next, Zoe climbed up on trembling legs and found a point on the catwalk where she could get a clear view of the drama below.

"Oh great!" she muttered. "How come this sort of thing never happens in the movies?"

Kendel was struggling limply. But clearly, there was no way that he could help himself.

"OK, so maybe it does. What would a movie hero do?"

Mind racing Zoe ran a hand through her hair and looked desperately for some other way to get down to the factory floor. He was struggling uselessly, trying to find some way to get off the machine and at least fall to the floor where he would have all the time he needed to work on the ropes that held him.

It was a good idea that wasn't working. The iron bar his legs were attached to was holding him firmly in place. She had to get down there fast and turn the power off!

Zoe was close to panicking when she almost tripped over a neatly stored role of chain. One end of this chain ran up to a block and tackle attached to a bar which was bolted to the ceiling. The other end of the chain was fitted with an iron hook hanging on the catwalk railing.

"Is someone up there?" Kendel called.

Zoe grabbed the chain and pulled. Plaster dust powdered out from one bolt. Trying to use this to climb down would be just as fatal as if she had fallen. Zoe thought of hooking the chain on the catwalk and climbing down that way when a strange idea struck her.

The press banged down then pulled up again and another set of chains pulled an empty bar holding its non-existent rug underneath the suspended wall of hot metal.

She was running out of time. The few minutes it would take to attach the chain safely to the catwalk and climb down had swiftly become much more than this man had to live. She had only one option. She tested the way the chain ran through the block. It moved like as smooth as a dream.

Kendel's voice drifted up from the factory floor.

"Look, you have to do something. My hands have been tied for too long. I can't move them. I can't get out of this myself. Say something, damn it!"

The press pounded again, accenting the man's mounting desperation.

It's you, Tolino, isn't it? Nick Tolino, you damn sadistic vulture you came back to watch!"

Zoe listened to these words with only a distant part of her mind. Her true concentration lay in the large metal hook in her right hand and the chain in her left.

Her body tingled with the effort of thinking out every move beforehand. As fantastic as it looked, this was her only option and there was no room for error.

Going out and down the fire escape, then finding an open door would take far too long. Even attaching the chain to the catwalk and swinging down on that way was impossible. She could do it if she had time but time here was running very short.

This was it. With the correct combination of aim, letting the chain go slack and then pulling it, her plan would definitely work. Maybe.

Distantly, Zoe realized Kendel had begun to say a prayer. It was a prayer for the dead. His hope was as dead as the still body on the cement.

Zoe forgot about him. She forgot about being lost. She forgot about everything except the desperate need to do this one nearly impossible thing.

The press lifted up. There were no other chains. No other invisible rugs to press. It was Kendel's turn to die.

CHAPTER 9

Zoe went back out to the roof, grabbed the valise and guitar as she went she climbed down the fire escape to the ground. There was a patrolman walking along the street immediately north of the factory. Zoe dropped her burdens on the sidewalk front of the building and ran, yelling for his attention.

"Officer! Officer! That building! Something bad is happening in there."

The man smiled at her in a fatherly way and when he spoke it was with a thick Irish accent.

"And now what would be happening in that old factory?"

"I don't know but there were sounds like gun shots and someone screamed."

The man's amused disbelief slowly faded. He didn't quite believe her yet but it was clear he didn't like the tone of her story.

"Gun shots you say?"

"Yes sir. You have to believe me. I'm telling the truth. Someone's in serious trouble."

He looked in the general direction of the factory.

"At least go and check it out!"

Slowly he walked the half a block to the front of the factory. Zoe followed him as far as the suitcase and guitar.

"Not to worry, Miss. You stay here. I'll see what's happening."

*****

Zoe leaned against the building across from the factory watching the scene with an even mixture of confusion and satisfaction. The patrolman had found the front door of the building locked and had walked out of sight around the side of the building. Once he was out of his sight she had quickly grabbed the guitar and suitcase then backed off to watch.

It was obvious he'd had no trouble getting in then finding first the victims both living and dead then a telephone. In less than ten minutes the quiet street had erupted into chaos. A morgue truck and an ambulance were now parked closest to the factory's doors. Adding to Zoe's confusion, both vehicles and the hand-full of police cars arriving in their wake fit in with the already established late 1920's early '30's theme.

Hovering at the edge of this official activity was a cluster of men carrying note pads. One held a huge camera. At first glance Zoe assumed that it was part of a television remote crew until she looked a second time and realized that it was a simple box-shaped still camera with a large flash.

The sight of this antique piece of technology gave Zoe a slow spinning feeling in the pit of her stomach. She was beginning to lose hold of her comfortable assumption that the dream which had brought her here was a dream. If it looks like a duck and walks like a duck and quacks like a duck, aren't the odds of it being a moose just a little slim?

Zoe realized now that Kendel was rescued, the investigating officers would come looking for her help in filling out their reports. They might even want to hold her as a material witness to attempted murder. She had to get away someplace quiet to think.

Grabbing the guitar case and valise, she started down the road away from the lake. No one else was around so she had claimed them for her own. A twenty-minute walk later found Zoe in a residential neighborhood.

She stopped to rest on a bench in a small park across from a school, putting the guitar on the ground and the valise on the bench. A few moments of restful quiet gave Zoe the strength to face the problem at hand.

She turned her attention to the valise. Somewhere there had to be a clue to where she was and how she had arrived here. She didn't believe in self-propelled flights through space. As for the rest of what lay around her, there was an explanation for everything. There had to be.

Defying her desire for explanation, the clothes and everything else inside the unlocked valise looked like the costumes and props from a period play. On top of everything lay a light wool coat. Zoe pulled this out and draped it over the bench.

Under the coat there was a quilted bag, tied with a ribbon, containing several pairs of stockings, two plain cotton bras, panties and a garter belt. Folded up under the lingerie bag was a small selection of dresses, a night-gown, a pair of low heeled shoes, and a leather clasp purse.

Under everything was a brown manila envelope containing a sheaf of what looked like legal papers mixed with photographs.

"Here we go just what's needed. There's got to be some clue in here. ID or something."

The first thing to come out of the envelope was a bill of sale. A property known as the Darby farm had been sold by a Miss Melinda Darby for ten-thousand dollars.

Along with the bill of sale was a death certificate for a Mr. Alan Darby. Another form dated two years earlier announced the death of a Mrs. Darby.

"Melinda Darby, I guess you sold the family farm and struck out for the big city. Where the heck are you though?"

The identity of the case's proper owner established, Zoe reached for the purse. Curiously the thing bulged so much that it threatened to burst its clasp.

What was stuffed into the purse made Zoe catch her breath. She didn't know if this was all of the ten-thousand dollars mentioned in the bill of sale, and she wasn't about to pull it out to count it, but it certainly looked close.

The only other thing in the purse was a wallet. Zoe took the wallet out and closed the purse, putting the bag safely back in the suitcase.

Inside the wallet, along with a birth certificate and a driver's license, was a small picture. The picture was a man and woman dressed in their best, standing stiffly side by side. There was also a newspaper clipping.

The story went into raptures over the talents displayed at the Ox County talent show. The contest had been won for the third year in a row by Miss Melinda Darby, playing her grandmother's beautiful hand-crafted guitar. Above the story a beaming Melinda stared out from the newsprint.

Every nerve in Zoe's body went suddenly numb. Her empty stomach did a half-twist and she shoved a fist in her mouth to stop the scream that threatened to erupt. The face staring out of the picture was her own!

*****

Kendel looked up at the iron wall suspended above him. He had seen it pause for a moment at the apex of its' movement, then come steadily downward six times. Lying immobile, he felt his fear had magnified that small pause into an entire lifetime. His vision blurred and his eyes drifted closed as his mind and body gave in to the enveloping heat.

He came to his senses slowly, through the magical power of touch. Cool strong hands lifted him off the hard flat surface. They removed the ropes and rubbed at his hands to help circulate his blood again.

Reason called it a wonderful dream until he realized he was being lifted from the cement floor and placed onto an ambulance stretcher. Confused, he opened his eyes to find a worried face hovering over his.

"Len?"

"You with us again, chief?"

"I'm not sure. I didn't think I ever would be."

This was impossible and yet it was undeniably real. The man kneeling on the floor beside the stretcher was Detective Len Barker. That meant he, Joshua Kendel, District Attorney, was still alive. Kendel licked his parched lips and managed a crooked smile.

"I feel like I'm in the middle of a really bad issue of TRUE DETECTIVE STORIES. The kind where the bad guy gets away, but the good guy some-how lives to fight another day."

Baker returned the smile and shook his head.

"You don't know the half of it boss. I was hoping you'd come to before they took you away so you could see this yourself. You'd have never believed me otherwise."

"See what?" asked Kendel.

"Take a gander at that."

Len stood and moved away from the stretcher so Kendel could see past him. The body of the man who had been his chief assistant, had already been removed. A police photographer with a large flash camera was taking pictures of everything in sight.

Of particular interest was the hook that had pulled the power switch away from its clasp. It was attached to a chain that was hanging from the roof near the catwalk at least fifty feet up.

Now he knew what the unknown shadow had been doing. He had been concentrating on a billion-to-one shot and he had beaten the odds.

"I'd like to meet the man who did that. I -- I knew there was someone up there, but I thought it was Tolino back to watch the blood spurt."

"I'm not so sure it was a man," said Len.

"What do you mean?"

"A girl in tight blue work pants and a strange baggy looking shirt and jacket told the cop on the beat she heard shots coming from this building. When he investigated he found you pulled you off the machine and called us. In all the confusion she slipped away."

He didn't get her name?"

"No. What she was saying seemed important enough to check out fast. It was too. The power might have been off but that piston was starting to slip. He pulled you out just in time."

"You're looking for the girl?"

"We have a notice out for her, but you never can tell with these drifters. The patrolman thought she was little more than a girl hobo."

"A girl hobo," muttered Kendel.

"Yup, carried a cheap valise and a guitar case. My guess is she'd been camping out on the roof to save the price of a bed. Lucky for you she did."

The room around Kendel began to move as the ambulance attendants wheeled him away. Len Barker walked along at his side. Kendel's mind began to move as well.

"I think I have to meet this girl hobo Len, and not just to say thanks."

Len Barker's voice was immediately guarded.

"You sure about that boss?"

"Yes. I know what you're thinking it's not exactly a friendly way to say thank you but, she needs to be found."

Kendel understood his friend's reluctance. He hated to put the finger on her, but if this "girl hobo" had been the one to do the trick with the hook, then she may have been witness to the fact that Nick Tolino had ordered him onto the machine.

That made her a witness to attempted murder. If he could keep her alive long enough to testify, he could put the biggest crime boss in the country away for a long time.

CHAPTER 10

"You all right, Miss?"

A man stood before her. He wore a blue janitor's uniform and his close cut hair was touched with white. It was a white that stood out like a faint halo against the deep ebony of his skin.

His eyes held a friendly concern and his mouth was turned up at the edges in a small kind smile. It was obvious however he intended to make sure she was no threat to the children now tumbling out the doors into the school yard across the street.

Zoe watched them for a moment, the boys were on one side of the building, the girls on the other. It was a separation that had gone out of fashion years before she had been born.

"Miss?"

The janitor was still there still wanting to know why she was here. The name sewn on his blue shirt pocket read JENKINS. The look on his face was almost as easy to read. No nonsense was going to be allowed. Straight answers only, please.

"I'm sorry. I'm a little tired."

As she spoke she began stuffing everything back into the valise.

"I've been traveling and I wanted to see if my things were all right. There are some pictures in here that have a lot of memories in them. Sometimes memories catch up with you at the funniest times."

"Yes, I guess that's the truth. I've had it happen myself."

Mr.Jenkins seemed to relax his guard slightly. The soft kind smile returned.

"You come far?" he asked.

"You wouldn't know it."

Zoe thought for a moment then remembered the newspaper clipping.

"It's a place called Ox County."

"You'd be surprised what people my age can know. I do know Ox county, pretty spot. I'll bet you hopped a train to save money didn't you?"

"Does it show?" she asked.

"Not exactly, but when you work in a school this close to the tracks you get into the habit of keeping your eyes open. You have to admit you're dressed a little funny."

Zoe didn't quite understand the comment about her clothing but she eagerly slipped into the role he was handing her.

"I -- I didn't want to dirty my good things. I do have money, but who knows how long it's going to have to last? It can be hard getting work if you don't know anyone."

Jenkins smothered a small laugh. He was completely relaxed now and appeared to be thinking.

"You know, I think that's the first common-sense thing I ever heard a girl your age say. Got a place to stay?"

Zoe shook her head thinking that not only did she not have a place to go she didn't know where to begin to look.

"Not yet. Do you know of any place that's not too expensive?"

"Miss Emily's home for young ladies."

Zoe's mouth fell open and stayed there until she managed to sputter out.

"Miss Emily's home for young ladies? You have got to be kidding."

"Now why would I kid about a thing like that?"

He seemed to be affronted by her reaction and she was immediately sorry for her slip.

"I'm sorry, Mr. Jenkins. It's just a kind of unusual name for a hotel."

It sounded like the cover name for a bordello, Zoe knew enough by now to keep that opinion to herself.

"It is a respectable boarding house," Jenkins said.

He'd fixed her with a sharp eye and Zoe began to suspect that he might have guessed what she had been thinking. The thought made her cheeks pink slightly.

"It's the best in the city. Miss Emily Houston owns it and my sister is cook and housekeeper there."

"Oh, I understand now. It sounds nice. Would they have room?"

"One of the girls just got married so I know there's a vacancy. You get a bedroom and meals for ten dollars a month. Gentlemen callers in the parlor only."

Zoe fought hard to hide her amusement at the phrase "gentlemen callers" and asked the next most sensible question.

"How do I get there?"

"Forty-two Spring Street."

He pointed in a direction that took her away from the lake and the factory with its cordon of police.

"You go three blocks that way and to your right."

Zoe thanked her benefactor, took up her luggage and started walking.

A boarding house for young ladies. It was a thing straight out of the old movies she had watched as a child. Perhaps this was a dream after all. Perhaps all this was simply the product of her over-active imagination. For the lack of any better ideas, Zoe followed the directions she had been given.

Her hands and shoulders soon began to ache from carrying their loads. A handful of cars drove past, each looked as if it had driven out of an old silent movie.

A candy wrapper pushed along by the breeze landed in the gutter near her feet. Next to it lay an empty cigarette package. Neither brand was the slightest bit familiar.

Zoe walked on and with every step saw some new detail that defied explanation, but it wasn't until she was standing in front of the huge Victorian mansion that the truth of the matter hit her. If this was a dream, and she knew it, then why hadn't she awakened by now?

If this was real, where was she? More to the point, where was home?

*****

Leaving the building Len barked orders to the men around him. A wall of big uniformed cops formed to push back the reporters so they could get the stretcher into the ambulance. Though it was clear to the watching reporters this man was still alive a part of the blanket covering him had been pulled up to hide his face.

"Who's the casualty, Len?"

"Barker, who do you have there?"

"Come on, Barker -- we know who the stiff is. Who's this? Come across, will you? We have deadlines to meet!"

"Its Kendel isn't it?"

This last loud guess caused a flurry of excitement that set Len Barker's teeth on edge. He surveyed the crowed with a look that made even the hardest of them step back to avoid his direct attention.

"Come on you boys know the rules. The injured party's name is being withheld pending notification of family. That is my first and last word, gentlemen. Good day!"

After a last icy stare Len Barker got in the back of the ambulance with his boss and the one attendant. The attendant banged on the barrier that separated the back from the driver's seat and the vehicle rumbled into motion. Len uncovered Kendel's disapproving face

"Len, you know how I feel about lying to the press. You start lying to the press they stop believing you. Then when you really need them, they turn their backs."

"I didn't lie Boss. I just didn't release sensitive information and you do have family that needs to be told," Len said.

Kendel groaned and said, "Oh Lord! I didn't think about that, Auntie Min is going to have a fit."

Len smiled at the battered man's momentary lapse into the purely domestic. He'd just stared death in the face yet here he was dreading the wrath of his widowed aunt.

Hoping he had the upper hand in the matter Len said, "Better she yell at you than cry on your head stone. Boss, you are still in danger and not just from your aches and pains. Although I have an idea you look worse off than you actually are."

Len waited for his boss to comment on this fact but the man laid out in front of him was still and quiet. His eyes, open just a crack, slowly drifted shut. Len looked at the ambulance attendant.

"He OK?"

The man held two fingers to Kendel's neck and watched his wrist watch for a moment.

"Pulse is slow but steady. I think he's just asleep. He looks like he bought himself a cracked head. Fading in and out tends to go with that."

Len nodded his understanding.

"I've had a couple of bumps like that myself. Listen, for his own safety we have to keep him as much out of sight as we possibly can. Where can he be looked at where we won't draw a crowd?"

The attendant's brow lined in thought.

"He'll need x-rays. Let me think about it."

Len leaned back against the van's wall and let the attendant think. He thought as well. He thought about the girl he had to find. He also thought about what had happened to witnesses in the past.

CHAPTER 11

A wide verandah ran around three sides of the house with well-tended flowering greenery decorating every inch. A small sign reading MISS EMILY'S HOME FOR YOUNG LADIES hung near the front door from two small hooks. There was no "Vacancy" sign. Clearly Miss Emily either relied on recommendations, or the room was already taken. Hoping that it was the former, Zoe crossed the street and pressed a large brass knocker into service.

A woman with a striking resemblance to Mr. Jenkins answered Zoe's knock. She stood in the door wiping her hands on her apron and looking Zoe over with an eye that missed nothing. Zoe endured the inspection as meekly as possible and was about to speak when the woman spoke first.

"Can I help you?"

She waited for an answer, her face showing only slight amusement over Zoe's choice of fashion. The older woman's costume could have fit any one of a dozen eras, a plain black dress with short sleeves and a hem line that went just below the knee, with a long, white no-nonsense apron. It wasn't exactly a uniform, but then this wasn't exactly a millionaire's mansion.

"Are you Miss Jenkins?" Zoe asked.

"I was once," she said. "How would you know my name?"

"I'm Zoe Darby. I'm new in town. I was resting in a park across from a school when your brother came over to talk. He recommended this as a good place to stay, that is if you have any room. He said you did."

"My brother sent you here, did he?" her eyebrows raised poetically.

"Yes, Ma'am."

"Well, my brother's an old softy at heart, but I guess you could clean up respectable."

The woman stepped away from the door allowing Zoe to enter.

"These things are just for traveling," Zoe explained.

"Miss Emily will be home in a little while. I'll show you the room so you can change. If she passes on you, then you have your place."

Talking as she went, the woman led the way through a large entry way and up a wide set of stairs, which turned at a landing. On the second floor she walked toward the front of the house and, after taking a key out of her pocket, unlocked a door.

"No men in the rooms ever. If you're keeping company, you can do it on the verandah or in the parlor. There's no cooking in the rooms. Over and above the mess it makes, those cheap hot plates are a fire hazard. If you want something, you come to me. Miss Emily likes to see the girls write home at least once a week. Just because you're all grown up and on your own, that doesn't give you an excuse to ignore your family."

"I may have a problem with that," said Zoe. "My parents died just recently. That's why I'm here."

"No other family?"

The woman paused, key in hand. Her face was a picture of understanding. No maudlin sentiment this, here was a person who understood loss. Running what she knew of this era through her head quickly Zoe fleshed out her family history for this attentive woman.

"The rest of my family died of the flu when I was little. Lawyers sold the farm out from under me when my father died. I was given what was left after expenses and debts and here I am."

"Well, God bless you, child."

She opened the door and led the way into the room.

"What are you going to do?"

"Get a job. I play this thing pretty well. If that doesn't work out I can type and I'm good with figures."

Zoe looked around at the room. There was a four poster bed tucked into one corner. A small sofa and two chairs were placed near a bay window where a huge piece of filigreed furniture with dials passed for a radio.

"Lunch is at twelve. Miss Emily should be back from visiting in an hour. I would suggest a bath and a change of clothing. Miss Emily doesn't approve of women wearing trousers no matter what the moving-picture stars do."

The older woman left, closing the door behind her. Zoe dropped her burdens on the floor and sank onto the bed. Obligingly the mattress molded itself to her body, its worn springs creaking softly.

Reality or dream, madness or simple nightmare, it didn't matter. Not when one gets right down to the bare essentials. This was the "elsewhere" Yolanda Wren had prescribed, and if the rules of mythic adventure were to be believed, even if she knew how to get back, that method would not work until she did whatever it was she was brought here to do. That rule established in her mind, Zoe relaxed and rolled off the bed.

There was time for a quick bath and maybe even a short nap before the meeting with the ominous Miss Emily, lady of the house. It sounded a little mundane, but after what had happened to her already that day, Zoe felt she deserved a bit of a break.

*****

The ambulance stopped but the attendant put a hand on Len's chest preventing him from getting out.

"I have to go talk to my partner. I think I know what we have to do."

He slipped past Len and left the van closing the doors behind him. Kendel shifted slightly in his sleep. Len laid a hand on the prone man's shoulder.

"Easy, Boss. We're almost there," he said quietly.

As if he heard, Joshua Kendel stopped moving. His breathing became deeper and more regular.

Len studied the sleeping man and knew from experience though he was badly hurt with proper care he would recover quickly. He himself had been injured once in war about the same time this man was entering college. He had been hurt again a few years later while still a uniform-wearing patrolman; beaten badly by the same sort of hoodlum who'd almost succeeded in killing this good man.

The small window in the wall between the driver's compartment and the rear opened up.

"I'm going to take you around to the rear. We'll go down in the receiving elevator to the morgue. There's an x-ray machine and pretty much anything you might need there. My partner's gone to talk to the head surgeon. He'll get him aside quietly and get him to slip down stairs."

"Great. The more out of sight we can keep him the better."

The driver started the van and they began moving slowly. Eyes on where he was driving he continued to ponder their problem.

"He's not going to be able to stay down there for more than a few hours. Sooner or later he'll have to go into a room," the man cautioned.

"Don't worry about that. When the time comes, we can take him home. He can afford private nursing and a doctor, no problem," Len said.

"No kidding? He's got that kind of money?"

"The guy's loaded."

"What's a guy like that doing messing around with gangsters?"

Len smiled. He wanted to tell this man that what they had here was the rarest of breeds. A rich man who cared and wanted to make a difference. He wasn't just the sort of man you wanted to work for, he was the sort of man you'd take a bullet for. But that was personal.

Instead he said, "My friend, if I ever figure out why he does what he does, I'll let you know."

CHAPTER 12

The bath tub was a small functional thing on raised claw feet. Curiously it was located in a different room from the toilet. That device had been placed in a space only slightly larger than a closet. Equipment located, Zoe coaxed a hot bath out of the shaky plumbing and briefly allowed the warmth to soothe her weary mind.

The bathroom window was open, letting in pine-scented bird songs and little else. No planes cut the silence with their high-altitude roars. Few cars rumbled past.

Somewhere outside a merchant called his wares.

"Fresh fruit! Vegetables! Eggs straight from the hen!"

Underneath that sound was the clip-clopping of a horse and the rattle of a cart providing a strangely rustic counterpoint. She didn't understand why he would be selling his things like that, but she liked the sound. After the bath Zoe attacked the problem of costume.

The clothing in the small suitcase was decidedly conservative even for this era. However it seemed to fit in completely with the aura of Victorian respectability the house seemed to radiate. A convenient coincidence made everything the right size, even the shoes, however there was a puzzling preference for very high necklines.

Feeling increasingly like a visitor from another planet, Zoe chose a white, lace-trimmed, blouse and calf-length brown skirt. After a frustrating wrangle with the garter belt, she got it right finally, although it felt as if she were wearing a lace-trimmed truss. Zoe stood in front of the mirror and marveled at the change.

"Wow, just like the picture in the newspaper clipping," she muttered. "I wonder..."

Zoe went to the dresser drawer where she had stowed the manila envelope and picked out the mixture of small black and white photographs that had been stuffed into it along with the legal papers. It was easily to spot Melinda. Her neck was covered wherever she appeared.

The answer to the puzzle was listed on the birth certificate that was folded up and stuffed into a pocket of the wallet. Under the heading of birth marks it listed a heart-shaped, port-wine stain on right side of the neck.

An odd idea ran through Zoe's head, causing her to catch her breath. Birth certificate clutched tightly in one hand she went to the mirror set into the closet door and undid the top three buttons of her blouse. No mark.

The sudden tension vanished and she breathed freely again. No supernatural hocus-pocus had placed her soul into the body of Melinda Darby. Whatever had brought her here had not taken that extra unbelievable step. She was simply a look-alike intruder, using Melinda Darby's things and planning to spend at least some of Melinda Darby's money.

Zoe did up her blouse and went back to the scattering of pictures on the dresser. They were stages of a life; some taken at fairs by traveling photographers. A few were in formal studio settings.

It was a life stolen, Melinda Darby's life. Zoe wanted to give it back, but where was the rightful owner? Where was Melinda Darby?

The echoing bong ... bong ... bong, of the grandfather clock in the downstairs hall drifted through the house, interrupting Zoe's musings. The opening and closing of the front door followed the sound almost immediately and soon after that came the woody creek of feet on stairs. Wanting to get things over with, Zoe met Mr. Jenkin's sister at the top of the stairs.

"Looks like my brother was right after all. You do clean up respectable."

Zoe found herself smiling weekly grateful for the vote of confidence.

"Thanks. It's been kind of a strange day, I forgot to ask what your name is."

"Alice Parks."

"Okay, Mrs. Parks, where do I go?"

Just for a moment Zoe thought she saw a mildly approving look in the older woman's eyes. It puzzled Zoe until she made a guess at the cause. She had called the woman Mrs. Parks, not Alice, a commonplace act of respect that had not gone unnoticed.

"She's waiting in the parlor. Follow me."

Zoe followed Mrs. Parks down the stairs and into a big room to the right of the entry.

"Miss Emily Houston, this is Miss Zoe Darby."

Mrs. Parks stood at the entrance to the parlor said her introductions, then left Zoe to walk into the room alone. For a moment Zoe felt as if she were in the middle of an old-fashioned play.

Miss Emily sat in a large high-back chair next to a fire place. A willowy figure in gray lace, she sat with back resolutely straight hovering an even two inches away from the leather chair's back rest. Her right hand toyed with a silver tipped cane that looked sturdy enough to be there for more than ornamental reasons. Her left hand held an exquisitely crafted crystal sherry glass containing a modest amount of amber liquid.

"You wonder at my breaking the law?"

"What law?" asked Zoe.

"Prohibition. I take a glass of sherry every day at this time and have done so, economics permitting, for much of my adult life. I will be eighty on my next birthday."

Miss Emily paused at this announcement as if she were waiting for some suitable comment. Zoe, who had never liked most of the things she had heard said about reaching old age, and couldn't think of anything else to say, said nothing. The old woman smiled slightly as if she were pleased by Zoe's silence.

"For the last few years this Prohibition insanity has made my little habit somewhat difficult to continue. Do you disprove?"

Zoe thought for a moment, gangsters with felt hats, cars with running boards, and now prohibition. It all fit together in a logical picture. As for Prohibition itself, she didn't have to work too hard to come up with an opinion.

"I've always wondered how they could justify outlawing something that has been legal for centuries. Cocaine and drugs like that are damaging even in small amounts, but alcohol only becomes damaging when it's abused, or if you're pregnant. No matter how many lives have been ruined by alcohol, banning it is no answer. Prohibition is a high minded experiment that failed, or rather is doomed to failure."

"How sensible of you to say so."

As if she suddenly realized that Zoe was still standing Miss Emily motioned toward a chair directly opposite where she was sitting.

"Do sit and tell me a bit about yourself. How long do you propose to stay?"

Zoe sat and told a swiftly concocted tale about how her widowed father had died leaving her the farm. Then a selection of suitably unpleasant lawyers entered the story saying that, as she was clearly unable to operate the farm alone, it would be sold out from under her. Her home thus disposed of, she was now in the big city to seek her fortune.

"You have money, then?" Miss Emily asked.

"I have traveling expenses with me. The rest is in a bank back home. I can wire for whatever I need. There's not much left after taxes and debts, but I should be able to last until I get some sort of job."

"And what sort of employment would you be looking for?"

"I have experience as a receptionist."

This was true, she had worked for over two years as part-time night receptionist for a courier company.

"I'd much rather get work as a musician. I play guitar."

Zoe swallowed hard wondering why she had spoken. It was an incredible notion. Yet on the whole the idea felt very right.

"You play well?" Miss Emily asked.

The old woman's plucked and delicately penciled eyebrows raised slightly. Her eyes took on a slightly cynical cast as she took a small sip of her drink.

"I've been told I play well, by people who know the difference," said Zoe diplomatically.

It was true. It was even a big reason why she had climbed out her bedroom window in the first place. But in spite of that support she never really believed she would try and make that dream a reality. People in her family did not become professional musicians. They played for their own amusement and satisfaction, then went on to do something sensible.

Miss Emily studied Zoe with a sharp eye. The longer she did so the thinner the mask of the Victorian gentlewoman became. Underneath was something else, something wild, attractive, and at the same time almost hypnotically familiar.

"Are you as innocent as your costume pretends, my dear?"

Suddenly Zoe felt as if she were playing a game of verbal chess. This woman was testing her and a successful mark meant more than simply a room to call her own. Thinking of the conversation that had taken place at Yolanda Wren's kitchen table, she wracked her brain for a suitable answer.

"I'm not experienced," she answered, finally. "But at the same time I'm not ignorant."

Miss Emily smiled just a little.

"Yes, I can see that. I can see that you have traveled and travel broadens the mind. I may be able to help you. I've been retired from business for some twenty years, however my interests were quite diverse. I still know many people. When I have something for you, I will let you know."

With that the old woman finished the remainder of her sherry, put the glass down on the silver tray on the table next to her chair, and stood with the aid of her cane. Her gray lace gown brushed the floor in a subtle echo of grander days. Without being sure why, Zoe jumped to her feet in response.

"You should enjoy the front room, it used to be mine. Alas, with this arthritis, I must avoid stairs. I sleep in a room off the kitchen. It's much warmer in the winter."

Miss Emily walked with the stately gate of a dowager queen toward a far door, which led toward the rear of the house.

"Few of the girls come home for luncheon, however I am sure that Alice can find you something suitable. You must excuse me for not joining you, I never take luncheon in public. I dine in my room and rest immediately after. Dinner is at seven, you will see me then. After we dine I am sure the girls would appreciate a little music. There is radio, but live music is so much better."

The door opened and closed and she was gone. A warm voice interrupted the silence that followed.

"She likes you. You're different. I'm not sure what it is, but you are different."

It was Mrs. Parks, standing at the sitting room door, a smile in her eyes.

"You were listening?" Zoe asked, making the comment more of a statement than a question.

"Of course I was listening. I have to keep track of things don't I? Her ladyship may own this place, but I run it."

"Doesn't Miss Emily object?"

"We go back a long time. She's taken care of me in the past and now I take care of her. And that's all you need to know."

"What kind of business did she used to be in? Was she an actress? She has that kind of grand aura."

Mrs. Parks smiled and an impish twinkle lit her eyes that had nothing to do with conventional business or the domestic world.

"I'll never tell," she said.

Mrs. Parks turned to leave. Zoe followed her out into the hall where she stopped at the bottom of the stairs.

"I'll be in the kitchen making lunch. Bed and board is ten dollars a month. You can pay when you care to. But remember, them what hasn't paid don't get fed."

"Yes ma'am," Zoe said.

She started up the stairs but was stopped by one last comment from the capable Mrs. Parks.

"I would take tonight's little recital seriously if I were you. It's none of your business who Miss Emily used to be. What she is right now is your best chance for a good future."

A little stunned from her unusual interview Zoe ran up the stairs and retrieved two five-dollar bills from the well-packed purse. After she paid the busy woman in the kitchen she returned to the room and counted the money. The bills had been rolled up in round bundles. Once counted, it added up to seven thousand dollars, most of it in tens and twenties.

It was a fortune that belonged in a bank, but that would have to wait until tomorrow. For now she placed one roll in a skirt pocket, hanging up in the wardrobe. The next roll went under a loose flap of lining in the suitcase. The next went into the dresser drawer and so on until the whole seven bundles were stashed so that only the most dedicated thief could find them all.

She then went down for lunch. This meal turned out to be a solo affair taken in the large dining room. Once her stomach was comfortably full and the dishes removed, Zoe found herself staring into space feeling something that was more than simple physical weariness. In fact was difficult to put a label on how she felt without sounding odd.

Was it jet lag? Dream lag? Interdimensional exhaustion? There hadn't been any time to rest before her meeting with Miss. Emily. Now that the meeting had passed successfully, it was about time she had that nap.

*****

It seemed to take an impossible amount of time before the doctor followed the ambulance attendant into the autopsy room. While he waited Len Barker pressed a phone sitting on a desk in one corner into use and organized a city wide hunt for the missing witness.

The doctor entered and nodded a greeting to the hovering attendant.

"Your partner's in the hall. He explained everything. I can take it from here."

The man left and the doctor, an older man with close cut gray hair and an attitude reminiscent of a military beginning to his medical career, turned to Len.

"My name's Hamilton Clay. You'll find my name on the front door as chief of surgery. I gather secrecy is our watchword here."

He turned his attention to his patient who lay motionless on the stretcher.

"Doc, the fewer people that know he's still alive the better. In fact I'd appreciate it if you gave him a shot to put him out for a while."

"If he's got a concussion that sort of thing might not be advisable. Why do you ask?"

"The longer I can keep him under wraps the better. The man who tried to have him killed thinks he's dead. That's too big an advantage to waste. The problem is he's not a very easy man to convince when it comes to laying low and resting."

The doctor smiled a thin smile.

"All right. I get the idea. I've been accused of something similar myself. You're a bit homely for a nurse but I've seen worse. Let's get to work."

CHAPTER 13

"What do you mean they can't find her!"

The hospital's basement morgue room echoed with Joshua Kendel's frustration. He had his shirt off and was sitting on the gurney on which he had formerly been sleeping. Doctor Hamilton Clay was in the process of taping his ribcage. Len Barker stood by the door.

"Okay, that's done," said the doctor. "Lie down on your stomach for a minute. I want to give you a shot for the pain."

Kendel grumbled, as he stiffly complied with the doctor's request.

"How come these damn beds are so uncomfortable?"

"I wouldn't know," said Dr. Clay, on his way to a far corner of the room to prepare the shot.

"The customers who end up down here don't generally complain."

As Kendel stretched himself out on the bed/table he found himself surveying the room. Of the five tables standing in a row only one other was occupied. That occupant lay still and cold under its thick rubberized sheet.

Kendel closed his eyes to shut out the still silhouette laid out waiting for attention. It didn't help.

In his minds eye, a hot iron wall floated a bare three-feet above his head, ready to flatten him into something that would take an autopsy and dental records just to identify. Sensing his superior's grim preoccupation, Len Barker filled the silence with the unnecessary details inherent in the problem of the moment.

"Boss, I started working that telephone the moment we got here. My men have been in and out of every rooming house and flop house in the city. They're checking the hotels now."

"They try Miss Emily's?" Kendel asked.

Len shook his head and waved away the suggestion.

"No point going there. That old woman only takes young ladies with at least three written references. There's no way she'd take a stray. I'm starting to think the girl must have hopped a train or something."

Kendel nodded in agreement.

"You have something there. Helping me out might have spooked her. Particularly if she is trying to blend in somewhere for some reason."

"I thought about that too. Mind you she could have family here. If she doesn't show by tonight I'll . . . "

"Start now!" Kendel barked.

He regretted the act immediately. His eyes flashed with stars of pain and for a moment his brain and stomach got together in an effort to decide if there was anything down there that could be convinced to make the trip back up. When he spoke again it was with much more respect for his battered head.

"Comb the countryside if you must. That girl is a material witness. If necessary I'll have her declared an unwilling witness and have her put under lock and key. But we have to find her first."

Dr. Hamilton Clay returned to the table brandishing an impressive looking syringe.

"All right son, let's see some cheek."

"I hate needles. Can't you give me a pill or something? I've wasted enough time lying around I have work to do."

In spite of his reluctance, Kendel inched his trousers down the required amount and lay still, eyes closed, waiting for the deed to be done. When the point did not plunge home immediately, he opened his eyes and looked at the two men who stood on either side of the table on which he lay. There was a message in their faces and for a moment Kendel was confused.

"Wait a minute what's going on here?" Kendel asked.

"You got to take a rest boss," said Len.

"I have to take nothing of the, OW!"

The needle struck home and almost immediately the sedative began to take hold.

"Insubordination, that's what it is, I . . . I . ."

Kendel tried to rise from the cot, but fell back. Gradually his pain stiffened body relaxed and in a few moments he was sound asleep.

"How long will he be out?" asked Len.

"Three hours," said the doctor. "He'd be better off with a full night or longer, but with that head of his I don't dare. By rights, he should be spending the night in the hospital. I wouldn't have done it at all but it's clear you're right. He doesn't do rest."

"By rights, he should be dead. I'd dearly love to announce officially to the papers that he is, then send him packing, but he's got this thing about lying to the press."

The doctor put the syringe away and turned to lean against the counter and study his sleeping patient.

"He's an honest man. If I remember correctly that's one of the qualities that got him elected."

Len said, "Yeah, I know. We'll have to sit back and let the rumor mill do the good work instead. Mind you, there's no way he'd be able to stay out of sight for very long."

"What will you do?"

Len gave a crooked and slightly fatalistic smile.

"Sit on him for as long as possible to give the cracks a chance to heal and then stand back."

*****

Zoe opened her eyes to the sound of four echoing bongs. She was completely rested now, but still had three hours to wait before meeting her housemates at dinner. When the memory of the suggestion of music tapped her on the shoulder, she rolled out of bed and reached for the guitar case, deciding to put the remaining time before supper to good use by tuning the guitar and warming up her fingers.

The instrument in the battered case needed very little tuning. It needed very little anything, except hands to give it voice. The newspaper clipping had said that grandmother Darby had built Melinda's unique prize-winning instrument.

Even if it had said nothing, it was clear that this was no product of a factory. Inlaid patterns of different colored wood almost sang by themselves the moment the light danced across the surface. When Zoe sat and prepared to play, the work of art melded itself to her body as if it had been made just for her or she for it.

An old wish came unbidden. A wish to dive into the music and let it become her life. A wish to escape into the magic of sound itself and never return.

With a will of their own, her hands began to move and music filled the room. Old familiar tunes danced across the strings. Only this time they were tinted blue and dressed in a minor key. Jazz, the music of old souls.

Her eyes blurred and she closed them as the sound filled her senses. This was not just music. This was life.

*****

A dissonant sound interrupted Zoe's world. She opened her eyes. The room spun for a moment and then became still. With a wrenching force of will she stilled her hands and brought silence to the room. Her fingers throbbed in the spots that had once been callused, but had gone soft.

Her whole body felt welded into one immobile form. Zoe tried to remember when she had played her own instrument for any length of time, but instead of a memory, her mind unearthed a dizzying revelation. She was good, but not this good, and she had seldom, if ever, played jazz.

You didn't become a jazz guitarist by force of will, or did you? She had willed the hook to catch hold of the power switch so that she could turn off the machine and save the man named Kendel. What had she willed just now? Had she asked her inner-self to produce music, music that would earn Miss Emily's patronage, or had it been something else?

A quiet knocking interrupted her meditations. Then there was a voice, hesitant and confused, bordering on worry.

"Hello? Are you all right?"

"Come in," said Zoe.

It was a young woman about nineteen or twenty years old.

"Hello. I'm Amy. My, but you're good. Miss Emily sent me to tell you that supper's on the table. She thought you might have lost track of time."

Startled, Zoe looked at the clock on the dresser. It said seven o-clock. Three hours after she had begun to play.

"I guess I did lose track of time. When I start to play, I tend to block out little distractions."

"I wish I could concentrate like that," said Amy. "I'll tell them you'll be right down."

Amy started along the hall to the stairs leaving the door open. Zoe slowly stood and walked to the bed where she had left the case. The light flashed off the varnished wood like a siren song inviting her to return to its nurturing power. Zoe closed the guitar into its case as quickly as possible.

She had grabbed for the old familiar freedom of music like a lost soul grasps at any symbol of home and a space of three hours had flashed by in what had felt like less than a minute.

CHAPTER 14

The first order of business the next day was to find a bank and rent a safety deposit box. Zoe had originally planned to open a conventional savings account, but one look at the date printed on the previous night's newspaper made her think again. JUNE 2, 1929, the year that her world had ushered in the time known in the history books as the Great Depression.

If this world followed her world as close as she was beginning to think it did, this was no year to put money in a bank account. In her own history the banks had failed sometime in the fall, she didn't know exactly when. She wasn't about to take chances, after all, this money wasn't actually hers.

The bank, recommended by Miss Emily, was a short ten minute walk away. Staffed only by men, it was a high ceiling and Roman-column affair, which took itself very seriously.

At first Zoe was amused by the almost ceremonial nature of the activity she observed behind the tall counter. By the time she was finally served, however, her sense of humor had worn very thin. It seemed to take them an inordinate amount of time to realize that she was not waiting for a bus.

When she actually was served, the clerk, a young man with a formal black suit and a high stiff collar, exuded a polished, patronizing charm she had never endured from anyone other than her father.

"Now, what's a pretty little thing like you need with a safety deposit box?"

"I need it to keep the family jewels of the last man who called me a pretty little thing," Zoe grumbled under her breath.

"I beg your pardon?"

It was hard not to laugh at the man's startled look. He had talked with her for all of three minutes, but it was more than long enough to feel his vision of what should be, begin to slip. Zoe gave him a wide smile and allowed him a small amount of pity. He simply didn't know any better.

"I have some family jewels I need to keep safe. I'm living in a boarding house right now and you can never be too careful, can you?"

He agreed, although his face betrayed the fact that her explanation did not fit with what he had almost certainly heard. Paperwork finished, he led her into the vault and left her alone to put what she wanted to into the box.

Zoe filled the small box with the legal papers that had been in the manila envelope, then squeezed in most of the rolled-up money. She pushed the box back into place then locked it and left the vault. Pausing just inside the vault door, Zoe looked out and saw the man who had served her. He was talking to another clerk and it was clear from his exaggerated movements what he was talking about.

It no longer mattered whether he knew better or not. Anger at the arrogant idiot's attitude overcame her desire for discretion.

To his right lay a table with two trays full of coins and bills that another clerk was rolling or bundling. On his left a broom leaned against the wall. Now was as good a time as any to prove to herself what she had hardly dared think.

The world faded into a momentary unnatural silence as Zoe focused all of her emotion-charged attention on the broom handle. Slowly, it began to move! At the same time, dimly as if in a dream she was aware that the clerk had noticed her staring in his direction and had taken a step away from the table.

It was far too late to stop. Behind him the broom first slid along the wall as if it were about to fall naturally, then impossibly, it stood up on one end as if were being held aloft by a string attached to the ceiling. The shock of success broke Zoe's concentration but she had already done what was needed. The broom handle came crashing down and in an instant the floor was covered in all manner of legal tender.

"Mr. Harris!" boomed an older man in the dead-still moment after the last coin had spun to a stop.

The hapless Mr. Harris stared across the room at Zoe, then down at the disaster all around him, then back at Zoe. This time, as they locked eyes for one split second, he looked as if he knew the truth. In that second his face revealed a superstitious fear she had never seen outside of television or film.

It didn't last. Fear vanished as doubt and confusion stepped in to assert their hold on reality. Zoe smiled, nodded a good day, and slowly left the bank. The bank manager's voice echoed in the ornately gilded rafters as she left.

"Not one copper coin had better be missing, Mr. Harris! Not one copper coin!"

Jubilant and afraid all at once, Zoe started down the street toward what looked like the city center. The next job she had assigned herself was to get to know the lay-out of the city and in turn develop an awareness of this world. Zoe was now absolutely certain that this was a different planet, perhaps even a different plane of reality.

Dinner at the boarding house the night before had been an event that was both formal and informal at once. She was given the feeling that she had been taken into a large family ruled by a grand dame who played the part of both mother and general of a carefully assembled team.

Once the dishes had been cleared away everyone but Mrs. Parks and the two girls whose turn it was to help assembled in the parlor. Here she had played a carefully controlled evening concert for her house mates. Mindful of what had happened that afternoon she had constantly forced herself to maintain eye contact with the people around her to avoid getting lost in the music.

After this she had sat in one corner of the parlor and read the newspaper cover to cover. Later in her room she listened to the radio until the station had gone off the air. The more she learned, the more she found that she had to accept the impossible.

Almost everything was as it had been on earth in the late twenties, and yet the differences were there as well. Place names might be spelled the same but were pronounced differently and in several cases the reverse was true. The country she was in was called America, but the current president mentioned in several newspaper stories was someone she had never encountered in any history book.

She was different as well. Somehow, subliminally, the people around her knew. The bank clerk had felt it long before she had conducted her little experiment. The day before, Mrs. Parks had actually said it, yet to Mrs. Parks and Miss Emily the difference was only one of spirit.

The real difference consisted of brain-stretching distance. Zoe Crane, alias Melinda Darby, was made up of matter from another part of the galaxy. That difference seemed the only key to the reason why she was able to do what she had just done.

The key to this power was emotion, desire, a deep need to do what was wanted. All she needed now was a reason to act and having acted, a method of finding the way home.

CHAPTER 15

Zoe walked until her feet throbbed. A tourist guide book from a store near the bank was now tucked into her almost empty purse.

The city, which called itself Chicago, was a medium-sized metropolis, proud of a recent manufacturing boom. This boom had given the city a museum, an opera house and large impressive looking stock exchange. The tour book claimed that this was a city with a bright future. Zoe thought they were probably right and wondered ruefully how much of that future she was going to have to see?

She had lunch in a small restaurant while reading a newspaper. The price of both paper and food made her realize exactly how much stability the money she had put away this morning represented.

At the same time she was struck with a bad bout of home sickness. The still dimly-understood words spoken in that far away kitchen echoed in her mind. She was here to experience life in a way that could not be experienced anywhere else.

It was intriguing and exciting, a new and different world complete with a strange supernatural power. All the same, as she watched the traffic through the dinner's window, remembering the fear that had flashed across the bank clerk's face, Zoe realized that she was very much alone.

After lunch Zoe took a taxi back to her new home. The prospect of more sightseeing had been dampened by the temperature, which had inched steadily upward since breakfast. The girls she had met over dinner the night before would be away at jobs or school, but at this point the only companion-ship Zoe craved was a softly playing radio and a cool iced tea.

"Miss Darby?"

Miss Emily's voice echoed slightly as Zoe passed through the entryway. Zoe turned away from the foot of the stairs and went to stand in the parlor door.

"Yes, Miss Emily?"

Miss Emily sat in her usual chair. Standing in front of the fireplace was a man dressed in a light gray suit and tie. His face, out of place with the civilized room and expensive tailoring, looked to be constructed out of bits and pieces of partially carved stone that didn't quite fit together. Miss Emily waved a blue veined hand toward her visitor.

"I have a guest I would like you to meet."

As the man's eyes focused on Zoe the rugged face slipped almost imperceptibly from quiet curiosity to something close to surprise. Zoe walked into the room, and an uncomfortable tingle began in the base of her spine. There was something about the way that he stood. She had seen someone stand like that not long ago.

"Zoe, this is Mr. Malone," said Miss Emily.

"You surprise me, Miss Emily," said Malone. "From what you said I pictured someone a lot older."

His voice, a mellow tenor, completed the picture. She had seen this man while crouching on a roof and looking through a broken window. This was the same Malone who had pulled the switch on a man named Kendel. Underneath his hard exterior it was clear that the man was not simply surprised, but puzzled, bothered by something that Zoe could not understand.

Miss Emily said, "Do not let her youth distract you, Mr. Malone. She is very talented."

Miss Emily looked from Malone to Zoe like a genteel referee waiting eagerly for something to happen. Zoe noticed her landlady's eagerness and took it as a cue. If some show of spirit was expected then she had better not be found wanting. She forced herself to smile at this dangerous visitor, and found the ease with which she did so surprising.

"Good afternoon, Mr. Malone. I've been out seeing the town. You seemed to have been talking about me."

"Zoe, Mr. Malone has an establishment," began Miss Emily. "Perhaps, Mr. Malone, you should explain."

"I run a place, members only of course,"

As he spoke his momentary confusion was forgotten and replaced with a comfortable smoothness.

"A Speakeasy?" guessed Zoe.

"That's it."

Malone eyed Miss Emily for a moment, then continued.

"It's got two rooms. The one up front is a restaurant with good food and drink, and in the back we got..."

"Gambling?" guessed Zoe. "What, no women?"

Malone's eye's narrowed slightly.

"You know for a kid fresh off the farm you got an awfully smart mouth."

For a moment the man's thin civilized glaze cracked, showing a glimpse of the animal underneath.

Miss Emily stiffened slightly, letting Zoe know, if she had not already guessed, that this man's tolerance level had been reached. Taking the cue Zoe offered Malone her most disarming smile.

"I'm sorry, Mr. Malone. I just wanted to let you know that I may be inexperienced but I'm not stupid."

Malone smiled and the glaze slipped back into place. He cleared his throat and laughed, as if he were embarrassed by his momentary slip. Zoe didn't believe the act for a moment, and from the look of her, neither did Miss Emily.

"That's okay, kid, just so long as we understand each other. The front room isn't big enough for a proper floor show, not if we want to make a good profit, so we have a trio playing while people eat. I figure to start off you could fill in while they take their breaks just for tips, you understand. The band might let you sit in with them, as well, but that would be up to them. After a few weeks, if you're still around, maybe we'll set up something else."

"Sounds reasonable," said Zoe.

"Eminently so," added Miss Emily.

"Good."

Malone took out a note pad and pen from an inside jacket pocket. He wrote on it.

"Here's the address to the club. The second door off the alley on the north side is the kitchen entrance. Be there by nine, I'll tell them to expect you."

He ripped a page out of his pad and handed it over. As he did so their eyes met, and for a single second the uncertainty showed again. Then with a snap the ledger pad was shut and both it, the pen, and any second thoughts he might have about her, disappeared undercover.

"Get some sleep, you'll need it."

Malone nodded a farewell to Miss Emily and left, retrieving his hat from an already hovering Mrs. Parks. At the sound of the man's footsteps disappearing down the outside walk, Miss Emily burst into laughter.

"Very good, my dear. Very good, indeed. Now you know his limits and he knows yours. He also knows that you are much too bright to be tricked into anything unseemly. Of course, that's not to say that he won't try again. Men do, you know."

Zoe felt suddenly as if her world had been tilted in yet another direction.

"So now I have a job in a Speak," she said.

Mrs. Parks entered the room smiling approvingly.

"It's not as shady as you might think. Many of the city's legitimate talent agents frequent Speakeasies. So do a lot of the towns more affluent citizens. So long as you stay out of the gambling room and drink nothing but soda water you should do fine."

"This Malone, he strikes me as a dangerous man," said Zoe.

"Oh he is, very," acknowledged Miss Emily. "You must keep both he and his associates at a strict distance. Use them, but do not allow yourself to be used by them, or you will be risking not simply your virtue, but your life."

Zoe wondered for a moment what Miss Emily meant by virtue, then she knew. She blushed slightly.

"I've always thought that one's virtue was a drastically over-valued commodity," said Zoe.

"Very possibly, my dear," allowed Miss Emily. "But believe me, taking foolish chances can have many different outcomes. I am quite old, and in all my years I have never known any way to over-value life."

*****

Zoe had very little time that afternoon for the nap Malone suggested. On the insistence of Miss Emily, she immediately went out again in search of something appropriate to wear for her professional debut. Mrs. Parks, had been given the job of seeing that she outfitted herself properly.

"Can you really call playing for tips a professional job?" She wondered aloud.

"If the talent is there, professionalism has as much to do with attitude as it does money," said Mrs. Parks. "Of course, the money helps."

"Money always helps," said Zoe.

They were in a fashionable dress shop looking through the selection of evening dresses. A deep blue strapless gown of shimmering taffeta caught Zoe's eye. She held it out for approval.

"How about this one?"

"That's fine if you're a headliner in the Zigfield Follies," said Mrs. Parks. "But if you wear that right now, you're going to spend most of your time doing the hundred-yard dash, and when you play games like that, sooner or later you lose."

Zoe, replaced the gown and continuing the search.

"We all lose sooner or later, and not all of us wait for the wedding night."

"All the more important to keep your head about it," said Mrs. Parks. "It takes careful planning to make sure occasions like that are remembered well. Now this is nice."

Mrs. Parks held up a dress that Zoe knew immediately was perfect. Made of a pebbled silk, it was a variation of the simple black sheath, with long clinging sleeves and a calf length skirt that flared for ease of movement. The scooped neck was lower than she had ever worn, and certainly far lower than the real Marion Darby would even think of wearing, but there was no doubt about it this one was perfect.

*****

"I've never seen a dress off the rack fit so well," said Mrs. Parks, as she served dinner that evening.

Miss Emily had announced Zoe's imminent debut that night at dinner. The other members of the household, seven girls in all, immediately deluged Zoe with questions. Uncomfortable with the attention at first, Zoe answered their queries as completely as her situation allowed. Gradually she came to realize that whether she succeeded or not, she was stepping into a life that was as foreign to these girls as this world was to her.

"What kind of shoes did you get?" asked one of the girls.

"Some flats with a kind of clear beading," said Zoe.

"Flats?"

"My grandmother doesn't even wear flats!"

"Why flats, why not heels?"

"I thought all performers wore high-heels."

"Not all performers have to haul around a big bulky guitar," explained Zoe. "If I played flute, I wouldn't need to worry. On the other hand, there's always the problem of running for the bus."

She eyed Mrs. Parks, who smiled in response.

"An altogether practical notion," said Miss Emily.

The old woman smiled benignly in Zoe's general direction. Zoe realized that Mrs. Parks had given a detailed report on the afternoons shopping trip. Normally upset about such things she realized that in this case she found this woman's interest rather comforting. It was care without limitations or qualifications.

"Now Amy, if you will say grace, we can all get on with dinner. Zoe will need time to dress before she goes to work."

CHAPTER 16

Joshua Kendel sat at his desk staring at the map of the city covering a large cork board on one of his office walls. After his short drug-induced nap, he had been smuggled out of the hospital and home. He had spent a night and a day resting as per doctor's orders, but once darkness had fallen he had insisted on coming here.

Only a small bandage covering a cut above his left eye, and the addition of three pillows cushioning his wooden office chair, betrayed the fact that he was still very tender after his business meeting with the city's underside. Feeling a need for a change of scenery, Kendel shifted his weight and looked to the opposite wall.

On this side of the room, Len Barker, special investigator for the chief prosecutor's office, stood looking out one of the three tall windows that showed the city itself. The man had a sour expression on his face, as if he were chewing on a lemon peel. His hands were stuffed deep into his pants pockets. A tinkling came from one pocket as a preoccupied hand jingled some coins.

"Why the hell aren't you on your way to California? You have more money than sense. Get on a train and go somewhere. There's a whole office full of dedicated people ready to take over. It's not just gangster against D.A. anymore it's personal."

Kendel shook his head.

"I know you mean well, Len, but I can't. At first it was just the liquor. No one said much out loud, not even me. The road to hell is paved with good intentions and Prohibition has got to be one of the biggest paving stones I've ever run across. If the hood's had stuck to poisoning damn fools with their bathtub gin, no one would have given them much more than a second look."

Caught off guard Len gave a small smile.

"I never thought to hear this sort of talk. You raided them right from the beginning."

Kendel shrugged.

"The law is the law. You don't have to like it to uphold it, but the picture's changed. Now they have gambling, prostitution, and the protection racket. For all we know they're probably starting to smuggle drugs."

Len pondered this last subject and shook his head.

"No percentage in doing too much of that. The market isn't big enough. Crooked or not these guys are businessmen."

"It could be," said Kendel. "These boys are in it for the long haul. If they find a way of introducing cocaine or opium or simple cannabis to their drinking clientele, ordinary people who are already doing something illegal for the fun of it, we could be dealing with a time bomb."

Barker turned away from the window and held his arms wide as if he were a preacher, preaching to the masses.

"Behold the prophet of doom with a price on his head."

"That price was collected last night," said Kendel, sharply. "They think I'm dead, or at least they have no reason to believe any different. Not yet."

"When do you plan on letting them in on it? You don't exactly have a low profile, you know. You've been out of sight barely twenty-four hours and already I've had almost two-dozen inquiries as to your whereabouts. Hell the news almost slipped out when we took you out of the factory. Sooner or later someone who's seen you is going to talk. You'll have lost whatever advantage you expected to gain from this . . . "

Footsteps echoed toward them from the other side of the closed office door. Len Barker pulled a revolver from a shoulder holster and stood behind the door, waiting. With an impatient wave of his free hand he tried to get Kendel to leave his seat, which was right in front of the door.

Kendel's only response was to pull his own gun. He cocked the hammer and placed the gun on the desk, muzzle toward the door. Kendel's private office was at the end of a short hall full of offices. At nine o'clock the offices themselves were empty. Even the cleaning staff had finished. In any case this firm, decisive step had nothing of the cleaning woman in it. This person meant business.

A man's shadow appeared in the smoked glass of the door. The silhouette knocked once, twice, paused, then knocked four times in quick succession. Kendel smiled and put his gun away. Watching this Len's mouth fell open in confusion. At the same time the door opened without permission.

The short, square built, man who stepped through the door was dressed in a simple dark suit, white shirt and black tie. In his hand he held a thin file-folder. The man's mild bookish face surveyed the room, eyes widening slightly as they lit on Len's gun.

"John Ludd," said Barker

He looked to the sky then over to the man at the desk as he put his gun back under his jacket.

"In person," said Ludd.

Ludd closed the door.

"Am I correct in assuming a little secret has been kept here?" asked Ludd.

Kendel answered this with deceptive innocence.

"Only because I've been too preoccupied getting patched up to mention anything. Then there was that unplanned little nap."

Len crossed his arms and eyed both men indignantly.

"It is my job to protect your battered body. Which taking into account the amount of co-operation I get can be a little tricky at times. Can we let Brother Len in on things now?"

"When this gang business began to get out of hand, I started making plans," explained Kendel. "Each plan was designed to fit a particular set of circumstances. The army does it all the time. John, as temporary head prosecutor, has been enacting plan X."

"What plan is this, pray tell?" asked Barker.

"We're going to raid Tolino's places," said Ludd.

"So what else is new?"

Ludd shook his head and smiled.

"This time is different. This time we hit them all, from the whore houses on River street on up to Malone's. We even got a contingent of state troopers on loan to handle the extra load."

"What about information leakage?" asked Barker.

Ludd shook his head smiling.

"The men were called in without being told why. Not only that, but each group is assembling in a different place. Even the team leaders think that their team is the night's only operation."

Kendel added, "That way, even if we have some information leak, they'll only move the evidence into the grips of another raid. Tolino's bound to get wind that something is about to happen. He won't suspect all-out war. I want on-paper evidence of the crimes these men have been committing. It has to exist. His operation is far too big to be run without some sort of written record. This is the only way I could think of that would work. I want Nick Tolino put away."

Ludd nodded in agreement, then said, "Before we do anything else, I have a situation that probably has nothing to do with anything. You'll want to know about it though, because it's more than a little strange."

"What is it?" asked Kendel.

Ludd put the file in his hands down on the desk. Kendel opened it and began to scan the few papers it held. As Kendel read Ludd explained matters to Len Barker.

"We found the body of a young woman stuffed into an old oil drum in the lane behind the factory where you almost met your untimely end. Thinking of the woman who had reported hearing shots I had Clancy, the patrolman the woman talked to, come in and see if he could identify her."

Len closed his eyes and cursed softly.

"What did he say?"

"He thinks it's the same girl but and here's the strange part. According to the coroner's preliminary examination, this girl has been dead nearly a week."

CHAPTER 17

A taxi dropped Zoe off across the street from the address written on the paper Malone had given her. The driver looked unhappy about letting her off alone on the dark empty street. He handed back the change from the bill she had given him, voicing his opinion at the same time.

"Miss, this ain't exactly a nice neighborhood. Are you sure you'll be all right?" he asked.

"A girl's got to do what a girl's got to do," she said. He stared at her, uncomprehending.

"Okay. I promise here and now to take a cab home."

The promise seemed to satisfy him. He put the car in gear and drove into the night. Zoe watched him go, feeling the residue of his warmth in the coins in her hand.

It was nice to be independent. It was also nice to be worried about. How one found a middle ground between the two conditions was a riddle for which she had no answer.

Zoe put the change away in the drawstring purse that had come with the dress, then reached for her guitar. Before she could move from the spot, a large luxurious car drove into a vacant parking spot across the street, two blocks along from where she stood. Watching the fashionable couple get out of the car, Zoe realized that she was about to be treated to a sample of how customers entered the club.

The man wore evening dress complete with top hat and silver tipped walking stick. The woman wore something very short covered with a satin cape trimmed in fur. They strolled along the street from where they had left their car, trying unsuccessfully to look inconspicuous. When they reached the building's unprepossessing front door, the man raised his stick and knocked; two quick taps, one knock, then three quick. The door opened and they disappeared inside.

The building they disappeared into was a large, square, bland, box-like structure. The two windows, one on either side of the door, were heavily curtained. There was an alley on either side of the building. Wondering which lane held the kitchen entrance, Zoe peered down the one directly across from where she stood and saw a door open somewhere near the center of the long stretch of darkness.

A man appeared, dumped a small bucket full of something into a large bucket full of something, then vanished into the building. Zoe crossed the street and started into the gloom toward the closed door.

Before she had gone far, another door closer to the street opened. A man in formal dress was tossed into the night with considerably less care than the kitchen help had taken when getting rid of the trash. The door then slammed shut. There was no outside handle.

Zoe examined the man who lay where he had been tossed. The cloud of alcoholic exhaust that hung about this over-indulgent customer was almost visible. Zoe left him where he was, grinning and mumbling to himself, and continued down the lane.

She knocked at the alley's second door. No answer. A louder knock produced the same results. It was getting late and since this door possessed a knob on the outside, Zoe tried it and found it was unlocked. Swallowing hard in a vain effort to still her nerves, she stepped through the portal and into the center of a whirlwind of activity.

Three men in chef's hats were giving orders in what sounded like six different languages while they served up at least fifteen meals at once. Tuxedo-clad waiters rushed in and out a set of swinging doors at something close to a dead run. At the same time, three men at a large sink dealt with the results of all this culinary industry in an attempt to keep the cooks and assistants supplied with clean tools to keep the cycle going.

Zoe stood at the door for a few minutes, wondering if there was a backstage and where it might be. Then she saw them. Like the calm in the center of a roaring tornado, three tuxedo-clad black men were taking their ease at a table in the far corner of the kitchen. It was set with what looked like supper.

Zoe guessed who they were and make her way through the kitchen. Suddenly very nervous she stood in front of them and smiled shyly.

"Hello, I'm Zoe Darby. Mr. Malone said that I could play in between your sets."

One of the men leaned back in his chair and studied her with a languid eye.

"Welcome Zoe, your coming was foretold."

"I'm Adam Smith. I play piano. The man sitting across from you is Morris Armstrong, he's string base. The third member of our little group goes by the name of Nathaniel Jackson."

"I suppose you're conservatory educated," said Jackson, dryly.

"Yes, but I don't specialize in the classics. I play in a variety of styles."

"I bet you do," said Jackson.

"Lay off the little girl," said Adam Smith.

He stood, took Zoe by the arm, and began to lead her through the kitchen toward the set of swinging doors, which obviously led to the dining room.

"Nat is self-taught," Smith said, as they walked. "He's a genius with a sax but some self-made men never understand that not all of us can get where we want to be on our own."

On the other side of the swinging doors was a wide, dimly lit, elegantly decorated room full of tables of various sizes. Set against one wall a stage with a baby-grand piano and a handful of chairs looked out onto a small dance floor. A fish bowl could be seen under the piano.

"Just pick yourself a chair, put the bowl on the piano and start. They'll get the idea," advised Smith.

"Where do they hide the gambling?" Zoe asked.

"See that door on the other side of the stage?" said Smith.

"Yes I see it."

"The customer knocks, then gives the password, or someone he's with does. When they let him in, first there's a little room where they feel them down to make sure they're not carrying any weapons. On the inside, there's gambling of all kinds and everybody's real friendly 'cause there's men on a little catwalk up near the ceiling. Each one of them carries a loaded submachine gun."

"Does this place ever get raided?" Zoe asked.

"Never has yet, but there's always the first time for everything. If something happens you just look for me or one of the boys. We'll see you get out all right."

He gave her a friendly smile and a gentle nudge in the direction of the stage. Zoe accepted the hint and let the man get back to his supper. She took the stage placed the tip bowl on the piano and began to play.

*****

"If it was her, she must have come back from talking to the patrolman and walked right into one of them."

Kendel's eyes stared hard at the road in front of the car. He was filled with a helpless kind of anger.

"They killed her just in case she saw something."

"Tolino does have a thing about witnesses," said Len.

"I didn't even get to say thank you. Now I have a dead drifter on my conscious and I don't have any identification to use so that we can track down whatever family she might have and let them know she's dead."

"I'll track 'em down," said Len Barker. "There's bound to be a missing person's bulletin out on her, if she's been missed. Even if there isn't, that's not the only way to trace a drifter. Anyway, it might not even be her. The coroner . . . "

"I know. I know. I just can't help feeling there's some kind of connection."

"You've been hanging out with me too long. Your turning cop."

Kendel closed his eyes and rubbed his throbbing temples.

"Maybe. Cop or DA, right now I am feeling miserable enough to insist on some answers. My body's sore, my head feels like it's ready to split open, and the pills the doctor gave me don't seem to be helping."

He let his hands fall into his lap. Instead of lying there loose they clenched into two tight tension-fed fists.

"You should be home in bed," said Len.

"I should be a District Attorney. Instead, I'm reduced to the status of pest-control officer."

The car pulled up in front of a large building with small carefully curtained windows. There was a brass plaque beside the door. It was too far to read but Kendel knew what it said.

"Malone's Fine Food and Music -- Members Only."

On the other end of the block, a truck with police markings pulled up to the curb and parked. The driver flashed his lights once, then turned them off.

For a moment the night was silent except for a rattling of garbage cans coming from the dark alley next to the club. To Kendel, it looked like a well-set stage ready for the curtain to go up. He got out of the car and closed the door in not quite a slam. Len did the same.

"Come on," said Kendel. "Let's go catch us some pests."

CHAPTER 18

Zoe guessed later that she had played at least ten minutes longer that she should have. Out of the corner of her eye, she had seen the three musicians at the kitchen door. Instead of signaling that they were ready to take over however, they simply stood by the door appraising her abilities. Clearly, they liked what they heard. Even the truculent Nathaniel seemed to give her more than a passing mark.

"You've got style, Princess," said Smith, as the three joined her on stage. "How about sitting in?"

Smiling widely at their approval she unloaded the tip bowl into her small purse.

"I'd like that, but I think I'd better listen for a while first. I need to test the waters a bit before I dive in."

Smith favored her with a friendly wink and a smile.

"That's all right, Sweetheart no rush. We've got all night."

He took his seat at the piano then turned to the audience and began to speak in a deep smooth voice that cut through the surrounding din with well-trained ease.

Twenty minutes later Zoe, who had taken an unobtrusive seat at the side of the small stage, had cause to regret her reticence.

"Me see flat-foot out front."

The man whispering the words was a middle-aged Asian bus-boy carrying a huge tray full of dirty dishes.

"Get out. Raid soon."

Thanking fate that they were due to finish soon anyway so their exit wouldn't be unduly noticed Zoe made a show of looking at her watch then slipping onto the rear of the platform that served as a stage. Once on the stage the easiest man to speak to surreptitiously was Morris Armstrong, the base player.

He listened, and, at the sound of the word "raid", immediately began a roller coaster of notes that at least three times had signaled the end of a number. The other men, sensitive to their fellow's every musical behavior, followed suit.

In the shadow of the applause that followed the end of the tune the base player quickly whispered Zoe's message. Adam Smith, his wide smile a little forced this time, turned and spoke to the audience as his colleagues packed up their instruments.

"Ladies and gentlemen, the boys and I are going to take a little break. But you stick around 'cause we'll be back in no time at all."

"I never liked this job anyway," whispered Nathaniel philosophically, as he passed Zoe on his way to the kitchen. "Them gamblers just don't appreciate good music."

"Double time, Princess," said Smith.

Casually, but with no wasted movements, Smith left the piano and led the way to the kitchen exit.

"From the sound of things, we maybe got about one minute to get clear."

Taking her free hand, the other held her guitar in its case, Adam Smith followed in the wake of the already vanished Nathaniel. Morris Armstrong, the fiddle player, lagged slightly behind, lugging his ponderous meal ticket with well-muscled ease. When they pushed through the swinging doors it was easy to see that the bus-boy had passed along the message of the impending visitation. The kitchen staff was gone, along with much of the readily portable food.

"Damn vultures never saved nothing for us," grumbled the base player.

"Aw, you're just sore you didn't make it back here fast enough," said Smith.

He opened the alley door.

"I get the impression you're used to this sort of thing," said Zoe, once they were outside.

"It's a fact of life."

Smith, peered in the direction of the open end of the alley.

"Nothing very bad happens if you do get caught. It's just inconvenient, and expensive. Come on, we'll go down to the other end of the alley.

There's a loose board in the fence. We slip through there and we're home free."

Zoe followed the men, confident in their friendship, yet something made her uneasy. She had a strange sense of going the wrong way for the right reasons. Something other than a raid was about to happen. Adam Smith's face fell as he stepped through the hole in the fence, straight into the beam of a bright flashlight.

"Ah, shoot," grumbled Adam.

A voice came from the other side of the blinding light.

"You men vanish,"

"You, Miss. I'd like a closer look at you, if you don't mind."

Smith whispered to Zoe apologetically.

"I'd stick around, Princess, but I got a family to feed."

"Don't worry," Zoe told the musician. "I think this was meant to happen."

Zoe stepped toward the light to find that it was held by a uniformed officer. It was an officer she had met before. He had been working day-shift when she had called upon him to rescue Kendel from his prison. Now he appeared to be working the night-shift, and of all the things that must be happening in this city, he had been assigned to this raid.

A clamor erupted from the building she had just left. The raid had begun. Instead of reacting to the noise, the man in front of her simply stared at her face.

"Great Sainted Mother of God! Miss, do you have a twin sister by any chance?"

Zoe immediately thought of the missing Melinda Darby.

"Not that I know of. Unless there's something my mother never told me."

The man looked grim and a little sad.

"I'm going to have to ask you to come with me, Miss."

"Why?" asked Zoe. "I just play guitar. You let the other musicians go."

"This is on a separate matter not connected with the business tonight."

It had to be connected to the affair at the old factory. That much was clear. The only confusing thing was his behavior. The man looked like he had just been presented with a secret and wished desperately for his lost innocence.

He led her to an unmarked police car parked in the front of the building, then sent a younger officer away with a message. Whoever the officer was sent to talk to must have been busy. Zoe had the time, and the unobstructed front-row seat, to enjoy the sight of almost two-hundred wealthy and not-so-wealthy patrons being marched out the front doors of the club and loaded unceremoniously into several police vans.

A second show immediately after the first was much more educational in its content. Over twelve boxes of what looked like business files were loaded into cars and driven away along with several grim, angry looking men.

Malone was not one of them. Zoe guessed that here in these boxes was the real goal of the raid and she hoped they found what they were looking for.

The young officer returned as the last of the gangsters was being driven away. He spoke to the older man who had stood silently beside the car awaiting his return. After this short talk, the older man got behind the wheel of the police car and began to drive.

"The person I want you to talk to, Miss, is the Chief District Attorney. He's a tad busy right now. I was told that I should take you to the city morgue. He'll meet us there as soon as he can."

"He wants me to identify someone?" guessed Zoe.

Zoe's stomach did a slow turn. Here was the reason this man had been so startled by her appearance. The reason that he had asked her if she had a twin. On this planet she did have a twin. That twin was the missing Melinda Darby.

"That he does," said the officer. "We'll just get ourselves off to the waiting room they have there and I'll see if I can find you a cup of tea. It's getting on past midnight and, to be frank, I could use a drop myself."

CHAPTER 19

The tea was hot and strong, and long finished by the time Zoe heard footsteps thumping down the hall toward the morgue's small waiting room. In the interim, Zoe had unpacked her guitar, filling the time with a selection of old Irish tunes that had totally captured her companion's heart. She stopped playing as the door to the small room opened.

"Making merry among the dead, Clancy?" asked Kendel as he entered.

"Well, no Sir. I . . . I mean we . . . that is, the young lady was simply passing the time."

Kendel smiled at the man's discomfort.

"Take it easy, Clancey. I know I took a while."

Zoe packed away her guitar then rose to greet Kendel, feeling her face go hot and flush. He was taller than her by about three inches; which put him at just six feet. She had known he was a well-built attractive man, that much had been clear even from a distance.

Now that they were face-to-face she could almost feel the energy that showed in every move he made. Here was a man who would achieve his goals, one after the other, without exception. Not one of those goals could possibly be anything less than earth-shattering.

"You're quite a talented musician, Miss. My name is Joshua Kendel, District Attorney. You are?"

"Zoe Darby."

"Well, Miss Darby, this isn't going to be pleasant, so we might as well get it behind us. Our friend, Clancy thinks there's a resident here that may be related to you. I haven't seen her myself. Shall we go and have a look?"

Kendel led the way out of the room and down a hall that might have been deliberately designed to reflect the somber nature of the institution. It wouldn't matter if it were midnight or high noon this passage would always hold the shadow of recent death.

Walking at Kendel's side, Zoe found her mind wandering to the thoughts of newly-dead spirits, lost, perhaps confused, lingering near their bodies for want of a better place to go.

Kendel paused at a door and knocked. Still thinking randomly of death, Zoe looked down the hall where they had come from. An image stood shimmering in the shadows. The image was a country colleen in silhouette, long flowing hair, a guitar in one hand, with just the hint of high button shoes and high lace collar. There was no mistaking who it was in the same way there was no mistaking the reason she was here.

"Is there something wrong, Miss?" asked Clancy.

At the sound of his voice the faint vision faded. A morgue attendant opened the door providing a convenient distraction as Zoe tried to shake the chill that had settled into her bones. Kendel took the door and waited for Zoe to enter.

"Of course something's wrong!" Zoe said with far more anger in her voice than she intended.

She stepped into the lighted room from the dark of the hall.

Speaking more reasonably she added, "If something wasn't wrong, I wouldn't be here."

Kendel closed the door on the face of the puzzled Officer Clancy, then turned to ask for directions from the attendant. The man gave Kendel the directions he asked for, at the same time handing him a clipboard. He looked oddly distracted as if he were unable to take his eyes off of Zoe's face.

Zoe sympathized. It was almost funny, but not quite. The room they had entered was a large one, filled with filing cabinet-like containers, two down the center of the room, and one on each end.

They left the attendant at his desk by the door, keeping his solitary vigil, and walked to a far corner. Kendel paused, his hand resting on one of the handles.

"This young woman was found hidden in a trash bin placed at the rear of a large factory. The coroner insists she cannot have been killed less than a week ago. I don't usually contradict the man, but if he's right, it makes something that I have a personal interest in rather difficult to explain. Perhaps you can make matters a little clearer."

With a slight tug Kendel opened the shelf, sliding it out until a sheet covered body could be seen from the waist up. A blast of cool preserving air stung Zoe's senses. It was a ghoulish reminder of the grim practicalities of life and death. Before Kendel could perform the service, Zoe reached out and lifted the sheet revealing the head and shoulders of the young woman who lay unclaimed, nameless, and alone.

It was a waxy expressionless face that looked up from its hard narrow bed. Paradoxically, this lifeless mask was crowned with a mass of curly auburn hair that glowed in the dim light with a life its owner had lost forever. The neck was covered in ugly bruises but not so covered that the large red birthmark could not be easily seen.

"I was left for dead inside the factory they found her behind. Clancy was on patrol two blocks away when a young woman he originally identified as our friend here ran up to him and told him that there was trouble. That's why I had problems with the coroner's verdict on the time of her death."

Zoe said, "You didn't know how she could have been dead a week and still have saved your life. Pretty good puzzle, you have to admit."

"You seem to know something about this," said Kendel.

"I think that's fairly obvious, don't you?"

"Who is she?" Kendel asked. "Are you twins?"

"No. Her name is Melinda Darby."

"And who was Melinda Darby?"

"A human being one of many," Zoe said.

Zoe covered the still face and closed the drawer with hands that betrayed her feelings with a faint trembling.

"So that's what I'd look like if I died tomorrow. Kind of interesting, in a gruesome sort of way."

Kendel interrupted her thoughts with a firm but gentle voice.

"You know, Zoe, you two wouldn't be the first twins to be separated because the family couldn't afford to feed more than one extra member. One of you must have been given up for adoption."

"I know that. I almost wish it were true, but the fact is you're wrong," said Zoe sharply.

"If you two aren't twins, who are you?" prodded Kendel.

"My real name is Zoe Crane."

Zoe felt a tear drip down one cheek. She wiped it away and swallowed hard.

"The rest is a very long story."

CHAPTER 20

Zoe was caught and she knew it the only real option was honesty. That option was not going to be well received.

"I woke yesterday morning on that same factory roof. I was the one who helped you out by doing the trick with the hook and chain."

"Quite a trick," Kendel said.

"I know. I spent so long looking for a stairway down from the catwalk there wasn't time to do anything else. After the machine stopped I ran to get Clancy. I was worried that if I just left you for the factory people to find the plunger might slip and you would end up getting flattened anyway."

"Why did you run off?"

"I was about to walk off with a guitar and a suitcase that I had found on the roof, I didn't want to get more involved than was necessary. I guess I was stealing from the dead."

"I think we can call it salvaging unclaimed property and let it go. Thanks for the help. How did you come to be on the roof?" Kendel asked.

Zoe opened her mouth and found that honesty was going to be a lot harder than she thought.

"I can't tell you."

The refusal confused Kendel.

He asked, "Why? You're not the first person to spend the night somewhere other than a bed."

"I know, the problem is, that isn't the truth. It may have been for Melinda here, but not for me."

Zoe pulled her eyes away from the closed drawer to look at Kendel.

"You don't think I killed her, do you?"

"No."

Kendel tapped the top-most paper attached to the clipboard the morgue attendant had given him.

"According to this, her neck is broken, and there are signs of other types of assault that are inconsistent with a woman perpetrator."

"You mean she was raped," said Zoe, bluntly.

Kendel looking away as if he were embarrassed by her frank understanding.

"Yes. Yes she was."

"Poor kid barely got past the rail-yard."

Zoe, placed a hand on the handle of the place where Melinda lay; needing to give sympathy yet having no living hand to hold.

"So much for chasing your dreams."

"Who are you?" pressed Kendel.

For a moment Zoe considered the question and wondered about her answer.

"I am a dream. I'm a mythic traveler who wants most of all at this point to go home. But I think I may have just found out why I was directed here in the first place."

"Why are you using the name Darby?"

"I had her identification. I don't know why we look alike, Mr. Kendel. Maybe God only has a certain amount of faces and he has to reuse them in different parts of the universe."

Kendel smiled.

"First you admit to petty theft. Now you're telling me you come from a different part of the universe. What next I wonder?"

Zoe looked down on the hand that she had placed on the drawer handle. Her watch was on that wrist and her watch was something that should not be there. At the same time it was her ticket to belief.

"If I told you in all seriousness that I am not from this planet, would you have me hauled off for a nice long rest?" Zoe asked tentatively.

Kendel appeared startled to find his joke taken seriously. He took a deep breath and let it go slowly.

"No, I'd be damn disappointed. But so long as you're not endangering yourself or anyone else, it's none of my business where you think you come from."

"Why would you be disappointed?" Zoe asked.

"You witnessed one of the most powerful crime bosses in the country order my death. If I could get you to testify, then I could put him away. However, it doesn't matter how co-operative you are, no jury in the world would convict a man on the testimony of someone who lists her home address as the second star to the right."

Zoe stifled a small laugh.

"Yes, I guess you have a point there," said Zoe. "Crazy thing is, as far as I can tell, it's the truth."

Zoe sipped off her watch. It wasn't expensive. The band was made of plastic squares held together by woven elastic. The face was a liquid-crystal digital display with a small flashing dot showing the passing of seconds. An ordinary, inexpensive, bit of ornamentation, yet inside the body of the watch was a small silicon chip, which could, with proper handling, take this vacuum tube era into the computer age fast enough to give it the bends.

Puzzled, Kendel took the watch from her outstretched hand. As he studied it his brows knit together in confusion. He held it to his ear. Then he looked at its width and examined the back.

"There's a battery inside," Zoe explained. "They usually have to be changed once a year."

"A battery?"

Zoe nodded and said, "They were invented for hearing aids originally. The batteries themselves are kind of expensive. If the watch is a cheap one, it's generally more economical to simply buy another. This one's a throw-away. I bought it because I liked the band."

The watch beeped and Kendel almost dropped it.

"Two o'clock and all is well," quipped Zoe. "Or is it?"

"There has got to be a reasonable explanation," Kendel said. "This is thinner than any watch I've ever seen. The workings would have to be minute. As for the face itself, that I have no explanation for at all."

"I come from a planet on the other side of the universe. I'm not entirely sure how I got here. I'd be more than willing to tell you the story, but I'd like to do it somewhere else if you don't mind."

96

Kendel tore his attention away from the watch in his hands and studied Zoe.

"Why?"

Zoe pointed in the general direction of Melinda.

"It's not every day you get to see yourself dead. Even though she's put away, just knowing that she's lying there with my face is beginning to give me the creeps."

"I'm glad you said that," said Kendel. "It makes you sound a little more human."

He held the watch out. Zoe took it, glad to be able to slip it back on her wrist, a small piece of home resting against her pulse. Its comfortable feel reminding her of a life far away.

Kendel said, "I'm good at puzzles. I received my Bachelor's degree with a science major and a criminology minor. Then, I went on to get my law degree. Even after all that, I'll be damned if I could tell you what material that band is made of or how the thing works."

"The watch itself is about fifty-years ahead of this point in time," said Zoe. "I'm not sure about the band. Can we get out of here please?"

Kendel nodded his assent and led the way back to the door. The attendant took back the clipboard and let them out, locking the door behind them. The hall was empty.

"That's odd. Where's Clancy?" wondered Kendel.

A cold shiver ran up Zoe's spine.

"I'm not sure I want to know."

There was danger here. Zoe didn't know how she knew, but at this point she could see no reason why she should begin to doubt her senses. Now was not the time to get curious. Now was the time to run like hell.

"Back door, fast!"

Kendel followed her down the hall without a word. To the right of the hall's end was an alcove with a door marked exit. Kendel grabbed the doorknob with his left hand, his right already in position of an impressive looking revolver.

"Locked," he said. "We'll have to get the attendant to let us out."

97

"No we don't," said Zoe. "We don't know what this is all about yet and at this point I trust that guy about as much as a mail-order diet pill. I can take care of this, you watch our backs."

After a split second of wondering about the best way to proceed, Zoe began to concentrate. Focusing her attention on one hand she began to think about the feel and look of the sort of key that might be used in the old lock. After a few moments of intense concentration, she could actually see the silhouetted image of a key in her hand. Zoe closed her fingers around the tingling slice of temporary reality, placed it in the lock and turned. The triumphant click of the opening lock was followed by Kendel's whispered exclamation.

"How the hell did you do that?"

"Good question," said Zoe. "If I ever find out, I'll let you know."

The door opened into an alley that ran along the rear of the building. Zoe was first out the door, thankful her black dress gave her a slight edge in the business of hiding in the shadows. Kendel closed the door softly, pointed in a direction with the muzzle of his gun, and led the way.

They had almost reached the corner of the building when there was a thud nearby. Something had been dropped onto the cement at the side of the building. Before they had time to wonder what it was, a strange voice provided a chilling explanation.

"You want me to finish him off, Boss?"

Another voice answered. This one was smooth, yet commanding, almost familiar. "Sure. Have fun. The noise will bring Kendel running, then . . . "

Before Kendel could react, Zoe jumped into the side alley. She never knew exactly what happened next. All she remembered later was the sight of a gun pointed at a huddled figure in a uniform.

"NO!!!"

It was a word that became a feeling, a massive force blinding her to anything but its own power!

CHAPTER 21

Zoe came to her senses on her knees beside officer Clancy as he lay on the ground. A man lay draped across the hood of a car parked at the mouth of the alley. There was no one else to be seen.

"Mr. Kendel?"

Silence, then the noise of shoes on pavement coming from the street. Zoe's heart pounded a few extra hard beats until Kendel's reassuring figure filled the mouth of the alley. He dropped down to one knee on Clancy's other side and checked the man's pulse by putting two fingers underneath the jaw and pressing gently.

"Will he be all right?" Zoe asked.

"He'll be fine. It looks worse than it is. They didn't have time to do much. They wanted to get him out of the way quietly so they could grab us as we walked out of the building."

Zoe felt her body shaking. She was limp with exhaustion as if she had just done something that had taken a huge effort.

"What happened?" Zoe asked, timidly. "I did something just now. What did I do?"

Kendel looked at her with blank disbelief.

"You mean to tell me you don't know?" he asked.

Zoe found herself fighting tears.

"Mr. Kendel I don't know what you think I am, but I couldn't do any of this until I came here. It was this morning before I understood what I was doing and that I could exert some sort of control. I am not some kind of Martian invader."

"I don't know what a Martian is, Zoe. But it's easy to see you're no invader," Kendel said quietly.

The ambulance arrived and so did a squad car. Zoe tried to stand, then stumbled. Kendel hurried to her side, helped her up. He led her out of the way of the attendants as they rushed to the aid of the unconscious officer.

"I have to take care of some business. You stand there and don't talk to anyone. We'll finish this little chat later."

Glad to have someone else making the decisions, Zoe did as she was told. Standing out of the way on the sidewalk she watched as the men loaded first Clancy, then the man draped across the car, into the ambulance.

While this was happening, Kendel spoke to two uniformed police. Near the end of the conversation he gave them a strangely shaped lump of black metal that he picked up off the sidewalk. The police tagged this strange artifact got into their car and drove off.

Kendel watched them go then went back into the morgue building then returned with her guitar.

"That lump I gave them looks very much like a melted

pistol." Kendel took a deep breath and let it out slowly. "I have a proposition to make and I want you to take it in the right way."

"Okay, shoot," said Zoe limply.

"We don't know if those men were after you, or me. It's possible they'll now be after both of us. I want you to move into my house. It's already under twenty-four hour guard. You'll be safe there."

"I don't know about that," said Zoe. "You could get me kicked out of my rooming house on suspicion of immoral conduct. Are you sure it's necessary?"

She meant the comment as a joke but it was easy to see the man in front of her took it seriously. Kendel shook his head. His shoulders slumped slightly.

"No, I don't, that's the trouble. Right now I'm tired enough to make mistakes and I don't want to make the mistake of sending you into harm's way. Dealing with these people is like walking through the jungle wearing a blindfold."

Zoe looked in the direction the ambulance had gone.

"Do you know who that was?" she asked.

"He's a cold-blooded killer. The problem is he's a freelancer. He could be working for someone, or he and his friend could have spotted me driving past alone and decided to collect on the bounty Tolino put on my head. Or it could be something else altogether."

"I think I broke his back," Zoe said, feeling squeamish.

"A pity it wasn't his neck. We've been trying to get the goods on him for almost two years. But willing witnesses aren't exactly common around here."

Kendel took the Zoe's guitar and put it on the floor in the back seat of his car, then opened the door to the front passenger seat. After a moments' indecision Zoe sat. It wasn't until they had been driving for a full five minutes that she spoke again.

"Well, what happened back there?" she asked.

"I was about to jump around the corner from the back alley when you moved out ahead of me. I heard you yell the word "No". After that, for about ten seconds, it was like standing just around the corner from a force-ten gale."

Zoe finished the picture. "When it stopped, you found me kneeling beside Clancy and that man was lying on your car."

"Exactly. While I was checking that you and Clancy were all right, I heard footsteps running and then a car start up and drive away. We'll know more when Clancy is able to talk, but from the sound of it there were only two of them. Presumably you got the one with the gun. By the way that morgue clerk is missing. I think they told him to beat it and he ran. From his point of view a sensible move. I don't blame him one bit."

Zoe thought back to the moment she had stepped around the corner.

"I remember seeing the gun. I felt anger and fear. I had to protect Clancy. I had to do something."

"How does this power of yours work?"

Zoe was almost grateful for the question. It forced her to apply some reason to what was swiftly becoming a chaotic mess.

"I have to need to do whatever it is very badly. Then I have to concentrate the emotional energy, focusing it toward some action. Like opening the door."

"And if you don't focus your energy?" asked Kendel.

"If I don't focus, I can get lost in whatever I'm doing. It happened once already when I was playing the guitar in my room. I got lost in the music and next thing I knew, three hours had passed."

"Well, you weren't out for hours this time. But it was a good five minutes before you knew where you were."

Kendel stopped the car in front of a large iron gate attached to a high stone wall and beeped the horn. A man holding a shotgun came to the gate and shone a flashlight at the driver's side of the front seat.

"Oh, it's you, Mr. Kendel. Hold your horses I'll have 'em open in a sec."

Zoe looked back after they had passed through the iron door. The man was closing and locking the gate behind them. When she turned her attention to where they were going her mouth fell open in surprise.

"Nice house," she said, marshaling her thoughts. "I think I once stayed in a hotel that was almost as big."

"I know'" said Kendel dryly. "Don't rub it in. I get enough comments like that from my staff. Let's just say I have a long string of ostentatious and conveniently successful ancestors. It lets me do what I want."

Kendel stopped the car in front of a set of bronze trimmed wooden doors that could have come from a castle belonging to a minor European monarch. He got out and walked around the front of the car, but before he could reach for the passenger door Zoe was out and standing next to him. Changing his course slightly Kendel retrieved the guitar from the back seat.

"Doing what you want almost got you killed," Zoe said.

She walked beside him as he led the way to the door.

"What I want is to get rid of these gangsters. I'm not a prude, but they're making sin big business. If we don't stop it, they'll eat this country whole and the remainder won't have enough goodness left in it to fertilize a petunia."

Kendel reached into his pocket, but before he could pull out a key the door was opened by a motherly looking woman in a robe and night-gown. A long braid of dark brown hair shot with gray hung over one shoulder.

"So, here you are, finally. If I told you that I've been worried sick and reminded you that the doctor told you to rest, you'd call me a meddling old woman."

"No, Auntie Min, I would not."

Kendel put the guitar case down just inside the door. Now that Zoe could see him in the light of the well-lit hall he looked very tired.

"Well, what would you tell me?" asked Auntie Min.

"I would tell you that I am about to take my medicine and crawl into bed. If you don't mind, Zoe, I think I'd better put off hearing your story until morning."

"Sounds good to me," said Zoe, thankfully. "I'd much rather talk to a pillow right now anyway. I'm asleep on my feet."

"Auntie Min, this is Zoe Darby. I would appreciate it if you would lend her a night-gown and find her a bed."

Auntie Min looked Zoe up and down. She pursed her lips crossed her arms and eyed Kendel.

"And why should I do that?"

He leaned against the door jamb for a long second took a deep breath then let it go.

"Well for one thing she saved my life the other night."

Auntie Min's mouth fell open. Taking advantage of the woman's stunned silence Kendel walked across the huge foyer and paused at the foot of a set of stairs wide enough to drive a car down.

"She did it again tonight and because of that, I'm not sure it's safe for her to sleep anywhere else."

CHAPTER 22

When Zoe woke the next morning she found the draw-string purse on the night table, but her gown, which she had left draped over a chair, was gone. In its' place was a beige cotton dress trimmed at the wrist and neck with hand-made lace. She had donned the dress and was putting on her shoes when, after a discreet knock, the door opened and a young woman in a maid's uniform entered.

"Oh, good, you're awake. Mrs. Kendel sent me to get you for breakfast. She doesn't think much of people who dawdle in bed."

"Mrs. Kendel?" asked Zoe.

"Mr. Kendel's aunt. She moved in when her husband died last year."

A long suffering expression let Zoe know exactly what was thought about that event.

"She's a good woman, but she does like things just so particularly meals, if you take my meaning."

The girl opened the door wide and stood waiting as if in a mute appeal for haste. Zoe finished putting her shoes on then led the way out of the room. The maid gratefully let the bedroom door close and was soon guiding Zoe along the second floor hall, down the stairs and along another hall that led to a room at the south end of the house.

"I must say, Miss, that fits you very well. It belonged to Mr. Kendel's sister. Lovely woman she was. She married six months ago and lives in Anglia. Though why she wanted to go all the way across the sea to find a husband is beyond me. Here we are. The food is in the warming trays on the sideboard. My name is Annabel. If there's anything you want, you let me know."

The maid opened the door and let Zoe into a beautiful plant-filled room with one wall made up almost completely of windows. Mrs. Kendel was already seated. Joshua Kendel was filling his plate from the sideboard. Zoe paused at the door, shyly surveying the scene.

"Good morning, Sleepyhead. I only just got here myself. Come on in and load up," said Kendel brightly.

The three covered trays holding breakfast yielded up, scrambled eggs mixed with smoked salmon, chicken livers and onions, strips of lean bacon and rolls that were so soft and warm they must have just left the oven. For a moment, Zoe wondered if she were in heaven. Reminding herself firmly that she didn't know where she was, and that it didn't really matter to begin with, she grabbed a plate.

"You look better this morning," she told Kendel.

Following Joshua Kendel's example she took a little bit of everything.

"When you went to bed last night you looked kind of blanched."

"I felt it. The moment I walked in the door everything sort of caught up with me."

Kendel, lead the way to the breakfast table.

"I collected a minor skull fracture and some internal bruising from that little business meeting you saw."

"What exactly did this heroic young lady do, Joshua?" asked Mrs. Kendel, her curiosity couched in ladylike restraint.

"I wouldn't call it being heroic," said Zoe. "They tied him to this big machine, turned it on and left. I was on the roof watching through a sky light. When the bad guys left, I snuck in and turned off the machine. Then I ran for help. Simple."

"Was it that simple?" Mrs. Kendel asked her nephew

Kendel's voice took on a tone that was just strict enough to make the older woman back down without starting a full-blown argument.

"No. But if Zoe wants to leave it like that, we will."

Mrs. Kendel's eyes widened indignantly, then her face settled into more comfortable conciliatory lines. She looked at Zoe and favored her with a maternal smile. For an instant Zoe was uncomfortable. The woman looked like someone with very definite ideas about the future who had no problem including anyone else in the fun.

"You're welcome here for as long as necessary, Miss Darby. Or longer, if you have no other plans. We are giving a little party tonight. I am sure you will find it most enjoyable."

"It'll be a nice intimate little gathering, including about two-hundred of our closest friends," quipped Kendel.

Mrs. Kendel was gently indignant.

"Now don't be like that, Joshua. If you are ever going to run for higher office you are going to have to start making some serious connections. If you will excuse me, Miss Darby, these affairs are a terrible trial. Such a lot to do and servants simply cannot be trusted to do things properly."

Kendel waited for his aunt to leave before speaking.

"My uncle was a senator. My grandfather was a congressman. My father spent two terms as governor. I even have a great grandfather that was almost a vice-president. She's determined that I follow in the family tradition."

"Do you want to?" asked Zoe.

Kendel shrugged.

"I may try it out of curiosity someday. My true interests are in crime and science. The two disciplines blend in ways that are just beginning to come to light and the whole thing fascinates me. Politics comes under the heading of things that I could do but don't feel it worth my while."

"Why don't you tell your aunt that?"

Kendel made a wide gesture of operatic frustration.

"I have, frequently. The problem is Auntie Min is what you might call a professional politician's wife. When my uncle died she lost her job, so now she's started in on me."

"Why doesn't she run for office herself?" Zoe asked.

The remark caught Kendel with a well-forked chicken liver hovering half-way between his mouth and the plate. Kendel let the organ hover for a moment, then lowered it to the plate. His eyes took on a half-serious, half-amused glint that Zoe found difficult to understand.

"Women do vote here, don't they?" asked Zoe.

"Yes, of course they do. Universal women's suffrage was granted in time for the last presidential election. I just never thought of it before. It might even be a good thing. My Aunt Minny in congress, running the country instead of trying to run me. I'd like that!"

The chicken liver on the fork jumped up, disappeared, and was chewed thoughtfully.

"Now that you've settled my family distractions. How about explaining away your own set of riddles?"

"OK, but I have to say right from the beginning that I don't understand most if it myself. As far as believing it, well . . ."

"You tell the story and let me worry about belief."

Kendel leaned back in his chair with a buttered bun and looked at her expectantly. Zoe took a deep breath and looked down at her hardly touched breakfast, wishing she had had a chance to eat more before this nervous tension vanquished her appetite. Another deep breath relaxed her voice and she began to talk.

She told him everything, from her problems with her domineering parents and the mysterious Yolanda Wren, to the boarding house, the bank, and finally the club. By the time she was finished, Kendel had downed his second cup of coffee and was looking out the wall of windows to the park-like grounds beyond as he analyzed her words.

In the following silence, a woman in a large white apron and white dress walked into the room from a side door.

"I am sorry, Sir. I thought you'd gone."

The words startled Kendel out of his reverie and caused him to jump to his feet.

"Not at all, Rose, we should have gotten out of your way long ago. Come on in and clean up. We'll take this little meeting into my office."

CHAPTER 23

Motioning Zoe to follow, Kendel led the way through the door she had used to enter the breakfast room and down the hall to another door. He opened the door and waited as Zoe entered first.

"This is my inner sanctum. No maids, cooks or aunts allowed without express permission."

"What, no gentlemen's gentlemen?" Zoe teased. She entered and Kendel followed, being careful to close the door behind him.

"Never. My father had a valet." Kendel shuddered slightly as if the comment had a long story attached to it, which he preferred not to relate.

"I'd rather dress myself."

"No wife?" Zoe added.

"I'd like to be married. I'd like children. The problem is I've always been a little too busy to do the socializing necessary to find a wife. I'm afraid most of the unattached women I run into in my line of work aren't the sort one usually marries."

The large desk in the center of the room was teak, the furniture was leather and the shelf-lined walls were full of books of every kind. A single narrow cathedral window of pebbled glass set in lead moldings allowed in light yet discouraged the inquisitive. Kendel slid into the chair behind the big desk and studied her.

Zoe sank into an overstuffed leather chair feeling truly relaxed for the first time since the adventure had started. It didn't matter whether he believed her story. Just telling it made a world of difference.

"You had all of Melinda Darby's identification. Why didn't you didn't open a regular savings account?"

"This world and mine seem to have somehow developed in a parallel fashion, with the important difference being we are technically and histori-cally more than seventy years ahead. For me, it's like going back in time. There are differences, quite a few actually, but they're subtle. It's as if the universe were a coin. On one side, there's my world, on the other side, there's here. Each one is different, and yet basically two halves of the same thing."

"OK I can understand that but it doesn't answer my question."

Zoe noticed he said "understand" not believe and smiled. He did seem to be taking her seriously but whether he believed the more impossible things she was saying was another thing altogether.

"On my world in 1929 there was a drastic stock market crash sometime in the fall. It had something to do with rampant speculation with no real money to back up the paper. Banks went under. Bankrupt millionaires jumped out of windows. People who were already poor starved. I wanted to protect Melinda Darby's money. I never did consider it mine. I wanted to find her. What happens to the money now?"

"It'll be a simple matter to trace her background and find out if she has any living relations. If there's no one to give it to then, as far as I'm concerned, it's yours."

"Less whatever it takes to pay for a respectable funeral," added Zoe, quietly.

"That part will be up to you. Last night you said you think you know why you're here. Why?"

"To find out who murdered Melinda," said Zoe.

"And do what?"

Zoe shrugged.

"I don't know. Make sure he's charged and convicted, I suppose. I'm no vigilante."

"You can act in defense for either yourself or others," Kendel pointed out. "You proved that last night."

"I know, but last night was not done deliberately. It was just a knee-jerk reaction to an emergency. I felt sick watching the ambulance take Clancy and that other man away. I felt like a freak."

"What are you going to do now?" Kendel asked.

"So far, I've simply gone with the flow and listened to my instincts. That seems to work fairly well. I may have a few extra tricks up my sleeve, but I'm not a detective."

"Whatever you are, I wish that you felt you were here to help me nail Nick Tolino. The man has built an organization so big and complicated that he ends up looking like a sterling citizen."

"Sounds like Capone," said Zoe.

"Who?"

"Al Capone, a gangster. He was a cold-blooded killer, but many ordinary people loved him because he knew how to manage his public image. The government ended up getting him on tax evasion."

"Tax evasion?" Kendel looked at her, stunned. "But if the man was a killer . . . "

"He was a killer, all right. I once saw a movie set in that era, where they had him sitting at this big round table having dinner with all his lieutenants. He gets up and walks around with a baseball bat talking about loyalty and team spirit then BAM, he flattened a man's head into the dinner table. I read later something like it actually happened."

"And they got him on tax evasion?" Kendel repeated. He stared across the desk at her with the same kind of incredulous look she had seen in the breakfast room.

"Look, the point is to get him out of circulation."

Kendel said nothing.

"Make it hard for him to run things."

Still he said nothing.

"Will you say something please!"

"Why didn't I think of that?" he asked.

"Probably because it was too simple. You or one of your staff would have come up with it eventually," said Zoe.

"Remember, for me this is history. On my planet a crime boss named Al Capone was jailed for tax evasion. He got the maximum sentence and was put away in the worst hole they could find. When he got out he was a broken man. He retired and died years before my father was even born."

"First you solve my family problems and next you solve my work problems. Are you sure you aren't here to help me?"

"No, I'm not. All I have is a feeling. I'm afraid I haven't had much practice trusting my own feelings. And, to be perfectly frank, I'm not sure."

"Is there anything that you are sure of?" Kendel asked.

"I have to move out of my rooming house and into your guest room. My being there has served its purpose. Going back to stay doesn't feel right."

"I'd watch that if I were you," said Kendel. "Auntie Min thinks every good politician needs a wife and I think she likes the way we look together."

He smiled at her in a warm self-confident way that said, although he wasn't about to let his life be run against his will, he also wasn't above co-operating with a certain amount of well-intended manipulation. It was a subtle kind of flirtation that made Zoe a little uncomfortable. At the same time, she was aware that his attention made her feel very warm.

"I'll take my chances if you will," she said, cheeks pinking slightly. "At any rate, I am really very poor wife material. The moment I do whatever I am supposed to do, I'll probably vanish in a puff of vapor."

A hollowness came over Kendel's smile that made Zoe wonder whether there was any part of her story that he actually believed. He had no choice but to believe the power she had displayed. The reasons for the power, however, were every bit as fantastic and her only proof was the watch she wore, an incidental bit of evidence that could easily be labeled some sort of trick and simply ignored. Telling herself firmly that his belief was not important, she continued.

"One thing I want to take care of right away is Melinda's funeral. I'd like to stop off at a funeral home and make the necessary arrangements."

"Sounds good to me," said Kendel.

The subtle flirtation had gone. He was now all business.

"Let's go."

"Wait a minute. Don't you have work to do?"

"I'm doing it. I am escorting and protecting a witness. After we do the right thing by Melinda, we'll go get your things from Miss Emilie's. Then I would like to drop by the hospital and have a few words with Officer Clancy.

CHAPTER 24

They took care of the funeral arrangements first. It was a tedious affair requiring a trip to a small funeral home close to the bank, then a trip to the bank, then back to the home to pay for the funeral.

Zoe was interested in how she would be received in both institutions now that she was escorted by an obviously important man. The result was as she suspected. At the bank they spoke to Kendel first greeting him almost as he walked in the door. At the funeral home even after he redirected their attentions to Zoe every one of her decisions was silently vetted by a glance toward Kendel.

Zoe knew that she should be annoyed but didn't feel like wasting the energy. It was a job that had to be done. When it was finally finished Zoe breathed a sigh of relief. Jane Doe number 6-B would be buried under the name Zoe Crane.

A small headstone would be placed on her grave with her name, dates of birth and death, and a harp. Zoe had wanted a guitar but that was as close to a musical instrument as the funeral home could come.

Stepping out onto the street from the somber gloom of the funeral parlor for the final time Zoe realized that Kendel was breathing a sigh of relief of his own.

"Not a big fan of funeral homes?" she asked.

"If you know of anyone who is, they'd better go see a doctor," Kendel said.

Zoe laughed at this and they started walking the short two blocks to where they had left the car.

"Crane. Is that really your family name?" asked Kendel, "That's it. The original version is actually something long and difficult to pronounce," Zoe explained.

"When my grandparents immigrated from Europe the immigration official couldn't pronounce it, much less spell it so he shortened it to Crane."

Kendel nodded his understanding.

"Interesting to note that simple-minded bureaucrats are a universal constant."

Zoe laughed.

"Actually, I'm glad he did it," Zoe said. "I can't pronounce the real one."

Kendel let her into the front seat of the car and then got behind the wheel. Zoe wondered for a moment why this man with a price on his head was traveling about the city without protection. She was about to ask when she noticed a blue sedan driven by two uniformed officers following at a discreet distance. Joshua Kendel might be headstrong but he was far from foolish.

"Now that the dead have been tended to we can head over to Miss Emilie's and pick up your things. I have to confess a certain amount of curiosity. That old girl has quite a reputation."

With difficulty Zoe pulled her attention away from their shadow to comment.

"I'm not surprised. Who is she? What's her story?"

"No one's quite sure. She showed up about sixty years ago. She was rumored to have been a prostitute and then a madam. If she was, it didn't last long because she soon started making a killing in the stock market."

"What do you mean a killing?" Zoe asked.

"It was almost as if she knew what stock was going to do well. She had an infallible instinct about what new inventions had potential and what were mere quackery. Don't let the rooming-house bit fool you, she only does that because she likes the company. That old girl's worth almost as much as I am."

Kendel turned the car onto the quiet tree lined street where the rooming house was located, and was immediately alert.

"Something's wrong."

Children stood quietly on nearby lawns talking in huddled groups, staring at the house. Mothers stood on verandahs talking in hushed tones. In front of Miss Emilie's Home for Young Ladies, sat a squad car and an ambulance.

"Oh shit!" Zoe exclaimed. "Miss Emily!"

She jumped from the car almost before it stopped. As she ran her vision blurred and a bitter lump built itself a home in her throat. On the verandah a blue uniform like a wall trimmed with silver buttons and a badge stepped out in front of her, speaking words she heard only distantly.

"Now where do you think you're going, young lady?"

"Let me go! I have to go in there!"

"D.A.'s office. Let her in," ordered Kendel.

Both the sitting room and the dining room were a shambles. After taking in the sad display of shattered finery, Zoe headed toward the kitchen at the rear of the house.

She stopped dead in the doorway. Mrs. Parks sat in a kitchen chair being tended by a stern looking man in shirtsleeves. A uniformed officer stood by a closed door.

She had stayed away simply to indulge Kendel's melodramatic sense of caution. It was obvious now that it had been a sensible move. Unfortunately it had been a move that had forced others to pay a price.

"What has happened here?" demanded Kendel.

He pushed past Zoe to enter the kitchen.

"Malone, that's what happened," said Mrs. Parks. "Him and two of his boys paid us a little visit this morning. They were looking for Zoe."

"Oh my, Mrs. Parks, I am so sorry," said Zoe.

"Not to worry, little girl." Mrs. Parks, shook her head gently and cracked lips managed a thin smile.

"It's a dangerous world. I've taken worse for much less important reasons. Once or twice for no reason at all. He wanted to know where you'd disappeared to and I didn't know, did I? No, it's better that you weren't here. Far better."

A sinking feeling settled itself on Zoe's shoulders.

"Miss Emily? Is she all right?"

Mrs. Parks looked away from Zoe's questioning gaze. Her eyes wandered from one unimportant object to another then, settled on the closed door.

"She's in there. I've never seen anything like it. They never laid a hand on her. They didn't dare. They roared around the house breaking things and yelling, 'Where is she,' but whenever they got near her they stopped. It was like she stood inside an invisible wall. The moment they walked out the door, she went to the telephone and called the doctor and then the police. Then she just keeled over."

Mrs. Parks looked back at Zoe.

"The doctor says she's been asking for you. Whatever happens when you talk to her, Child, remember; this is not your fault. She's been living on borrowed time for longer than you've been alive."

"Living on borrowed time?" asked Zoe. "Or living here on borrowed time?"

Mrs. Parks' face froze, then she looked away. When it became clear that she would say nothing more, Zoe walked to the door, took hold of the doorknob, then stopped.

She wanted to speak with the old woman, ask her the questions that had been forming in her mind since that first strange interview. But when questions are asked, there are often answers, and answers could sometimes be more difficult than ignorance.

"You don't have to go in there."

It was Kendel who spoke, breaking the vague haze that had settled over her mind. His hand rested on her shoulder with comfortable solidness. His caring banished the unreal reality to which she could not afford to surrender.

"I need to know something. There's something about her. I saw it from the beginning but didn't understand."

Zoe pushed open the door. The old woman lay as if in state. Two of the girls who lived in the house, and whose names Zoe could not remember, sat by the bed. It was difficult to tell what was wrong, perhaps it was simple old age.

"You can go now, Girls."

The deep gravelly voice startled Zoe, making her notice that the man who had been treating Mrs. Parks had followed them into the room. Zoe sat by the bed in a chair given up by one of the girls. The doctor waited until the bedroom door had closed out the world before he spoke.

"I don't know why this didn't happen ten or even twenty years ago. It's almost like a stroke. Yet, when she wants to speak she can quite clearly."

"Is there nothing we can do?" Zoe asked.

"Keep her comfortable and wait for nature to take its course. I'll be in the kitchen. Call me if you need me."

The doctor nodded his head slightly and left the room. Zoe placed a hand on one of Miss Emilie's. The fragile skin felt feather thin and had the look of a flower petal at dawn. The bones underneath this delicate covering had the feel of weathered twigs. Death danced here and life. Soon one of them would bow out.

"I'm here, Miss Emily. It's Zoe."

The old woman's petal thin eyelids opened revealing the shadow of the fire that still dwelt within its frail home.

"My mother was a whore and a drunkard. I never knew my father. If it comes to that, she never told me if she knew him in any way other than in the Biblical sense. She died when I was fifteen. I won't tell you about the years in between. But by the time I reached twenty I was quite done with life.'

"I remember going out of the dirty little room I lived in and sitting on the railing of a bridge that ran over a shallow river. I was trying to get up the nerve to dive in head first."

She stopped but Zoe knew the pause didn't come from weakness. It came from memory old and powerful.

"Something happened didn't it?" Zoe asked.

"There was a post beside me. On top of the post was an old-fashioned round street lamp. The bulb was burnt out, yet as I sat there a glow began. The glow called to me, offered me a chance. I reached for that chance and it pulled me here."

"Did you ever meet a woman named Yolanda Wren?"

"No."

"Was there anyone standing near you on the bridge?"

"No, Yes! There was a woman. A woman was walking along the river. She was the reason I looked away from the river; the reason I found myself looking at the lamp. She looked so beautiful, so calm, walking there in the moonlight. I didn't want to disturb her peace. I was going to wait until she had gone then jump."

"Did you ever see that light again?" Zoe asked.

"Once. I turned away from the light and made a home here instead. I can only assume it respected my decision for it never came again. I know I have never regretted my choice."

"You know what I am. What should I do?" Zoe asked.

"Do what you must."

The old woman's eyes drifted shut and the room was silent for a time, the only movement being the shallow rise and fall of the fragile breast. When Miss Emily spoke again it was as one half asleep.

"I knew you for a fellow traveler from the moment we first met. We were the same and yet so different so different. You were all so very different."

The old woman's last breath came in a rattling sigh that rose and then fell away into nothingness. Zoe stood reluctantly and stepped away from the bed and toward the door. It was time to leave.

The room she had slept the one night in had been searched with little regard for personal property, but nothing had been taken. Packing everything that had not been destroyed into the small valise was the work of minutes. In the entry way she found Mrs. Parks covering a mirror with a dust cloth.

"My grandmother did that when my grandfather died," said Zoe. "She said it was to prevent his spirit from getting caught in the glass. You don't strike me as a superstitious type."

"For everything there is a reason," said Mrs. Parks.

"Sometimes it's as simple as giving you something to do."

"Where does her money go?" asked Kendel.

"Good sized lumps go to my brother and cousins. Most of it goes to me. My grandmother found her walking the streets like an empty shadow. She didn't have a penny in her pocket. My mother and her got to be like sisters."

"Did she ever tell you where she came from?" Zoe asked.

"She did. Mother and I were the only ones she ever told. Well, she may have told my gran but we never spoke of it. Last night she told me that you came from there too. Are you going to stay long?"

"I don't know," Zoe said.

Mrs. Parks started to walk into the parlor, before she could leave the entryway Zoe spoke again, stopping the woman in her tracks.

"Did you believe it? Her story?"

Mrs. Parks swallowed and set her jaw as if she were about to say something very hard. When she turned back to Zoe there was a sadness in her face that had nothing to do with the natural grief it replaced.

"No. I never could," said Mrs. Parks. "Down through the years there have been young people. She would help them and sometimes she'd take me aside and say, 'That one's a traveler, I can see it in the eyes.' After a while I got to be able to see it too. That's why I let you in."

Mrs. Parks looked around at the shattered finery and a tear dragged its way down one cheek.

"She had money, friends, even a kind of family if you count the girls, who've lived here over the years. But she was never happier than when she was helping her travelers."

Mrs. Parks stood for a moment deep in thought. Zoe watched her think. It looked as if the woman were feeling a pain that had nothing to do with the beating she had taken or even the loss of her lifelong friend.

"It makes me sad to think she knew I didn't believe her. I think she did know. If you will excuse me, there's a lot to do and I'd like to get it done before the rest of the girls get home."

CHAPTER 25

"Now you want me to believe Miss Emily Houston was sent here from your world as well?"

Conversation, as Joshua Kendel drove the few miles from the rooming house to the hospital where Clancy lay recovering, had been terse to the point of open argument.

"At this point, Mr. Kendel, you can believe what you like. Most people do anyway," Zoe said sharply.

"What did she mean when she said you and she were different?" Kendel asked.

Zoe stopped feeling angry. In place of her anger was loneliness.

"I think she meant that I have a reason to go home. All she had was a reason to stay."

"Why do you have to go home?"

Zoe wracked her brain for an answer to the simple question but found none.

"I don't know. I've been too busy to think about it."

"Well, don't run off before tonight, I'm going to need a dance partner."

Zoe gritted her teeth and looked out the window, vowing to say nothing more until they got to the hospital. The man sitting beside her was handsome, intelligent, and wealthy into the bargain. At the same time he had a slightly superior, even smug, way of communicating his growing interest in her that made her teeth tingle.

*****

"Officer Clancy is doing well," said Dr. Hamilton Clay, as he led them down a white-washed corridor.

"I'd have sent him home before now, but I'd like him to take it easy for a day or two and in the man's own words, 'There's very little ease to be found in a home with six children.' He's in that ward, fourth bed on the right."

The room they entered had ten beds, five on each side. Officer Clancy was sitting up with a studious look on his face and a racing form in his hands.

"Clancy, I'd never have thought you a lay-about," said Kendel playfully.

"It's been a terrible trial, Sir, but it is doctor's orders," said Clancy.

He set his racing paper down on his lap and waited for the questions he expected from his visitors.

"OK you know what I want to hear. How did it happen?"

"I heard a man call down at the other end of the hall. I thought that they were delivering someone and were having trouble getting the stretcher through the doors. I went down to offer my assistance when I got there . . . "

He shrugged and gently prodded a bandage that covered part of his head, evidence of the skull fracture the doctor was concerned with.

"That's how I figured it happened. I made a call the clerk came in this morning and made a statement. He was handed a five dollar bill and ordered to leave. If he hadn't taken it he would have got the bad end of a gun so I don't think we can blame him much," said Kendel.

"No indeed sir," said Clancy.

Kendel asked, "Who were they? We have Henry Angelo, but at least one other was heard leaving the scene."

Clancy's open friendly eyes clouded over.

"Henry Angelo, you say?"

"You were lucky," prodded Kendel. "I understand that it probably happened very fast, but you must have caught at least a glimpse of someone. Enough to make an educated guess."

Clancy shook his head and shrugged his shoulders.

"That's what Mr. Ludd said this morning when he came to take my statement," Clancy said distantly.

"What did you tell him?" asked Zoe.

"I remember a wind, a great rushing wind."

"Do you remember why you were at the morgue in the first place?" Zoe asked.

The man in the bed opened his mouth, then closed it and simply shook his head. Kendel looked to Zoe then at Clancy.

"You were on patrol two mornings ago. Do you remember anything unusual that happened?" asked Kendel.

"Now that's a daft question. I pulled you off that machine. I had to break into the factory office to use the phone and call for help."

"How did you know to go in there?" asked Zoe.

"I . . . I . . . " Clancy's brow knit together in concern. "I should know."

"A passerby?" offered Zoe.

"That's it!"

Clancy, smiled widely as if a load of worry had been removed from his clouded mind.

"A night-shift worker on his way home heard something odd and told me. I looked into it and found you as they left you."

Kendel looked pointedly toward Zoe.

"Yes, I suppose that must have been it. Take care of yourself, Clancy and thanks again. I'll see you around."

Following the signs on the white walls that led to the wing where the criminal, Henry Angelo, was being kept, Zoe could tell Kendel was very close to being extremely angry.

"What was that all about?" Kendel asked.

"Isn't it obvious?" said Zoe. "He can't remember me."

"I don't suppose you had anything to do with it? You realize, don't you, that this eliminates yet another witness?"

"I'm sorry, but I didn't do it. Not on purpose at least!" exclaimed Zoe.

"Maybe it has something to do with what I did last night. Personally, I'm not sorry. The fewer people who know I'm walking around with a dead woman's face, the better I'll feel."

A uniformed officer stood outside a door, letting them know that they had reached their goal. Kendel showed his identification and they were granted entrance.

The room was small, holding a single bed. The man in the bed did not move. He stared at the ceiling, his face a blank.

"Well, Mr. Angelo, it's time for a little talk," said Kendel.

The man in the bed reacted to the sound of Kendel's voice, but in the silence as Kendel waited for an answer, he returned his attention to the ceiling.

"Come on, Henry, wake up and smell the coffee."

"I don't think this is going to work," Zoe muttered.

She swallowed hard, willing a wave of nausea to pass. There was strangeness about this man's blank, unthinking face. There was something wrong here that went far beyond any physical damage.

"It has to work," said Kendel. "We need to know who he was with."

Kendel grabbed Angelo's chin with one hand and turned his face so that they looked each other in the eye. He then leaned over the bed speaking in clear forceful tones.

"You and I have to talk, Angelo. Who were you with last night?"

Angelo simply looked at questioner. His gaze held all the mental force of a flower pointed toward the sun.

"Stop that!"

The forceful voice of an angry floor nurse interrupted the unsuccessful interview.

"I will not tolerate that sort of behavior in my ward!"

Kendel turned to the nurse speaking with a force that startled Zoe and for a brief moment unsettled the nurse.

"You'll damn well have to until this thug starts talking!"

Sure of her facts the nurse answered Kendels claim with the cold truth.

"The man cannot answer. I'm not entirely sure he understands. If you had asked me his condition earlier, I would have told you."

"Brain damage?" guessed Zoe.

"Yes, the doctors believe so," said the nurse. "They don't know the cause of it, but what you have there is a man-sized infant. Actually, he's worse than an infant. A true infant spends all his waking hours trying to gain the knowledge that it will need in life. He just lays there."

"What are you doing about it?" asked Kendel.

"We have a therapist beginning to teach him how to feed himself. He shows some interest in his surroundings when it comes to food, but if you want to know about something that happened before he arrived here, you're out of luck. Unless I am seriously mistaken, that life is completely lost."

CHAPTER 26

Joshua Kendel drove his house guest home. Once he had seen her safely in the front door he drove on to his office. As he entered the building's lobby, he was greeted like a conquering hero by a mob of reporters.

"Mr. Kendel how close are you to charging Nick Tolino?"

"Any truth to the rumor you're ready to pull Malone in?"

"Mr. Kendel are you fully recovered from your injuries?"

Kendel stopped at the lobby's main stairwell climbed a few steps up so that he could be seen by all that were there and turned to speak to the group.

"Gentlemen you will have to give my office time to analyze the information we have gathered. Believe me. When we are ready to act you will know. So will Tolino. As for my own condition. I'm a bit battered and bruised but I'm still here. I'm ready to give the gangsters in this town a real fight."

Joshua climbed the stairs while behind him a handful of officers escorted the reporters out of the building. When he entered the large open room that housed the main workings of the District Attorney's office he enjoyed a second more personal welcome.

Trading quips with his staff regarding his underworld brush with death, and the massive raid, which it prompted.

"Hale the concurring hero."

"I knew you were too tough to kill boss!"

"Welcome back boss."

"We'll get em this time Boss no two ways about it!"

His secretary, a middle aged woman normally as tough as the men she worked with actually hugged him.

"Gawd help me I'm so glad to see you in one piece. I swear I was a mess when I thought we'd lost you."

"Lady and gentlemen your good wishes are welcome. I don't think I need to remind you however that one of our number did not survive that little meeting. I don't think I need to remind you which meeting. Let's get to work on this evidence and see if we can put his murderer behind bars."

Kendel silently motioned a summons to Len Barker and John Ludd. The two men followed him through the cheerful crowd to a door on the far side of the room. Once through the door, they walked down a short, door-lined hall and into Kendel's private office.

Once the office door was closed, Barker said, "I've been hearing some strange reports of your activities after the raid last night, Boss."

"Yes," added Ludd. "I'd like to hear this story myself. Clancy wasn't much help. Most of his memory of what happened last night leaked out the crack in his head."

Barker leaned his compact frame against the windowsill turning his back on the view of the city. Ludd, the last through the office door, closed it, then stood at ease in the center of the room, hands in pockets.

"Why on earth did you go to the morgue in the first place?" asked Ludd. "What's more to the point why did you go without your tail?"

Kendel settled carefully into the pillow lined seat behind his desk.

"They were busy and I felt this was important. Remember the puzzle we were talking about before the raid? I thought the hoods in this town in general would be a bit too preoccupied to bother following me around. Turned out I was wrong."

"Was this about the dead girl?" said Barker.

"Officer Clancy apprehended her mirror image sneaking out of the back alley behind Malone's."

"He what?" asked Barker.

"She was sneaking out the back with the club's musicians. Her hair is a lot shorter and she is without the birth mark, but even if you take that into account the resemblance is striking."

"There's our puzzle solved. Kind of oddly coincidental but they do happen I suppose," said Ludd.

Kendel smiled and shook his head.

"Oh it gets better. Knowing I'd want to see her, Clancy put her in a car then had a patrolman track me down while he kept an eye on her. I told him to take her to the morgue and that I would meet him there, which I did."

"And that is where the toughs caught up with you," said Barker. "What happened to Clancy?"

Kendel opened his mouth to explain, then shut it.

"I'm not exactly sure. I didn't see it."

"Who is she? Where does she come from?" asked Ludd.

"Her name is Zoe Crane, but she's calling herself Zoe Darby. She plays guitar. After that, it gets a little complicated. She's the one who saved my life by doing that trick with the chain and the hook. She did it again last night, but I'm afraid she can't be called for official questioning."

"Why?" exclaimed Barker.

"She has a fake identity and a history that would never stand up in court. She'd end up going to jail for perjury and Tolino would walk away laughing. The problem is if she told what she says is the truth, she'd be committed."

"There goes our attempted murder conviction," said Ludd. "Our first gold-plated witness and she turns out to be a fruitcake."

Kendel cocked his head in the general direction of the main office.

"How goes the paper battle?"

Ludd said, "It's going to take us a while just to figure out what's there. Once we know what's there, then we have to figure out what we can use."

"Locate the ledgers, they're the key," said Kendel. "Find out where the money goes. If we can prove a sizable undeclared income then we can send the bastard away for tax evasion."

Barker's jaw dropped and would have hit the ground were it not firmly attached to his head.

"Tax evasion!" gasped Barker. "The man's a murderer!"

Kendel smiled broadly. The fury of the man in front of him was almost comical.

"Tax evasion carries a maximum sentence of ten years," said Kendel, "which is better than having him out and active. Wouldn't you agree?"

126

"Yes, I would," pondered Ludd. "I think it could work. It would take time, but it gives us something to look for. Excuse me, I want to spread this idea around."

The door had been closed behind Ludd for some minutes before the exasperated Barker managed a comment.

"What are you planning to do with Malone, send him to summer camp?" he asked.

"The books state quite clearly the maximum sentence for tax evasion. What they don't say is where the sentence has to be served. Ten years on Rock Island should be enough to take the wind out of anyone's sails."

Barker contemplated his superior's words for a moment. A thin smile and a slight twinkle in his eye advertised his growing understanding.

"You know, Boss, you're getting pretty devious. I like it. Where is this Zoe now?"

"She's moved into my house," Kendel said.

Barker's brows rose in unspoken surprise. Answering his chief investigator's unanswered questions, Kendel went on to detail the events at the morgue, downplaying the supernatural element as much as possible. He continued with a straight forward account of the morning's events. When the tale was finished he simply leaned back in his chair and waited for the curtain of disbelief to fall. It did so without delay.

"You don't believe any of this fairy story, do you?" Barker asked. "It's got to be some sort of trick."

"I believe Zoe Darby saved my life twice. How, I'm not sure. I believe someone ruffed up that old woman's cook and pushed the old woman into a fatal stroke. The cook says it was Malone and two of his boys. I believe her too."

"With Malone, I'd believe anything."

"As for Zoe like I said, she's a guitarist, a good one, I heard her play at the morgue. She was filling in the time until I could get there. Apparently the old woman knew Malone and pulled some strings to get Zoe a job playing at the club."

"Why does he suddenly want to find some girl guitarist?" Barker pondered. "You'd think he'd be more concerned about the raid."

"It could be one of two things," offered Kendel. "A: he thinks Zoe is a police agent whose presence was somehow connected to the raid. B; her appearance troubles him. Having seen the dead girl and her living counterpart side by side, I'm not surprised. Now that she's dropped out of sight, that's going to trouble him even more."

"You connecting him to the Jane Doe?" asked Barker.

"We know that Malone thinks himself a real ladies man," said Kendel.

"The crumb never met a real lady in his life," grumbled Barker.

"Exactly," said Kendel. "What might happen if he found a nice girl fresh in from the country who'd snuck away to a secluded spot to grab a small nap?"

"Just about anything," said Barker. "Wait a minute! The body was hidden, but, according to your girlfriend, the valise and the guitar were left out in the open. That's not like Malone. Too messy."

"Distractions. The man has to keep track of his own club and supervise Tolino's whole operation. Anyway, if his finger prints aren't on them why do anything at all? Malone's no fool. If anything he's smarter than his boss."

Kendel reached for a file that balanced on the top of his desk's well-packed IN basket.

"How long is this nutty house guest of yours going to stay?" asked Barker.

"As long as I can convince her to. She's got some funny ideas, but she says what she thinks. And, in a woman, that's rare. Sooner or later she'll tell me the truth about who she is and how she does what she does. Then we'll see what we can see."

"Be sure to let me know when the big day is so I can get my Sunday suit out of the cleaners," Barker quipped.

"Mr. Barker, whatever do you mean?" Kendel asked innocently.

"You've got that look in your eyes," said Barker.

"That, maybe it wouldn't be so bad to have a woman run my life, look. I've seen it before."

"Don't you have work to do?" asked Kendel, pointedly.

"Plenty. You going anywhere today?"

"No, I'll be in all day."

Kendel eyed his paperwork with a martyr's expression. Barker saw his bosses' expression and laughed.

"Then tonight there's that party," said Kendel.

"I know. I've already set up the extra security," said Barker. "I'll be there myself at eight sharp to supervise."

"You don't have to, you know, not that you aren't welcome but as a guest. You've pulled a lot of hours lately. When was the last time you got a full night's sleep?"

"If I remember correctly it was the night before you got elected," said Len.

The two men laughed and Barker opened the office door. He paused at the open door for a moment as if searching for something to say.

"Boss, look, I know you think I worry too much. Maybe I do. But I'm alive. And after all I've done, that counts for something. If Tolino wanted you dead before last night in my book right now he wants you even deader. I don't think he'd be above barreling into your place and mowing down half the city's upper crust just to get you."

"Tolino's too smart to do something that open."

Len shook his head grimly.

"When a smart man gets mad he does stupid things. There isn't a fortress that's ever existed that hasn't been breached at least once. That house of yours may be big, but it's no fortress."

CHAPTER 27

Not knowing how to contribute, Zoe spent most of the day watching the staff under the direction of the remorseless Mrs. Kendel bustle about putting the already splendid home into party readiness. Late afternoon found her hiding in her room strumming the guitar and contemplating the situation at large.

There were either an infinite number of possibilities or only one. Melinda could have been killed by a passing tramp. If you eliminated that wide open field, then there could only be one candidate, Malone.

His poker face had cracked the moment she had walked into the parlor. He was far too pragmatic to think her some sort of ghost; the girl herself risen again to exact revenge. Even so, Malone wanted to find her. No doubt to ask, without the conventional social constraints, exactly who she was.

At five o-clock Annabelle, the maid who had called her for breakfast that morning, came in with a light supper on a tray. She carried the tray in and set the dishes out on a small table by the window. The young woman looked exhausted and was more than ready to exchange a few words with someone close her age.

"It's a good idea, hiding like this. I wish I could. The florist is late with the flowers and Her Majesty is in a right old snit. I sponged your dress down so it's nice and fresh. I'll bring it up presently so you can change. No hurry though. No one ever shows up at these dos until eight."

*****

Zoe watched the first guests arrive from the shadowy safety of the top of the stairs. The scene was like a genteel sort of dance; ritualistic, repetitive. Yet each time she greeted a new arrival Mrs. Kendel would behave as if the whole affair were happening for the first time.

"Good at what she does, isn't she?"

Zoe jumped at the sudden voice at her shoulder, then looked up at Joshua Kendel in crisply-pressed formal wear, smiling warmly. She smiled back and found herself enjoying his obvious approval.

They stood in the shadows admiring each other, oblivious to the growing crowd who continued to arrive. A high-pitched matronly laugh broke the spell, causing self-conscious giggles on both sides.

Zoe returned her attention to the scene below.

"All she has to do is change her script from 'How do you do, my dear,' to 'You will support my bill, won't you?' She'll be a natural."

"Shall we join the uncommon rabble?" he asked, offering her his arm.

"Might as well. After all, I'm dressed for it."

Zoe took his proffered arm reluctantly and they started down the long curving stairs.

"Who am I? What I mean is, who do we tell them I am? We can't tell them the truth. I'd end up feeling like a sideshow freak; The girl who saved the D.A.'s life."

"I know. I've already talked to Auntie Min about that. You're Zoe Darby, niece of an old friend. She's taking on the job of showing you about and introducing you to people. In fact, this whole tiresome affair has turned into your unofficial coming out."

Zoe blinked twice at Kendel's last statement. Coming out? debut? Those were terms that belonged to a distant time where the moneyed few discreetly arranged for their sons and daughters to marry within their social circle instead of marrying some stranger without an iron-clad pedigree or at least a suitable bank balance. Zoe had an idea that on her world, in certain small circles, this sort of thing still happened, but it would never have happened to her.

It took almost two hours for her to wish that it hadn't happened at all. It was impossible not to enjoy walking and dancing with her handsome companion while the cream of the city's upper crust looked on with admiration. It was during the breaks where she occasionally drifted away from Kendel that she began to feel the irritating social constraints of the position into which she had been put.

131

The men, who gathered in groups to talk of politics or business, would change the subject completely whenever she approached. The women would constantly comment on what a wonderful couple she and Kendel made, what a lovely dress she was wearing, or she must come to so-and-so's place for the weekend.

As the night wore on the whole game of saying polite things to strange people began to wear very thin. Here, men's and women's worlds were very different. It wasn't something with which she could feel comfortable. Then she took a closer look at the six-piece band and got a pleasant surprise.

"Hello, Princess," said Adam Smith. "I wondered if you were going to drop by."

"I've been rushed here and there all night. I only just had a chance to inspect the music. Mrs. Kendel has good taste."

"Nope, not her. We work for Mr. Kendel. Her ladyship wanted a string quartet, but Mr. Kendel put his foot down. It is his money after all."

"My guitar's upstairs. What's the chance of taking you up on your offer and sitting in?" Zoe asked, innocently.

The piano player's kind eyes grew shadowy and a little sad. He finished the piece he was playing, giving the end flourish an extra blue twist, then looked at Zoe.

"Little girl, I don't know how you ended up here and I don't want to know. That's your business. I just want to give you a little piece of advice. You sit in with us tonight and they'll never think of you as any better than one of the help trying to pass as quality."

"Quality? I don't understand."

He smiled sadly.

"I know you don't. I like you even more for it. Give them a chance to know you as one of them. Once they do, then you can bend the rules. Until that time, you stay on your side of the stage and we'll stay on ours."

"That's not fair," said Zoe.

"Child, I know it."

Zoe watched as the long tapering fingers played a sanitized, civilized version of a tune they had played at the club. Elevator music, except elevators here didn't have music in them. As Zoe listened to Adam Smith's music, another man's work began to run through her mind. The man's name was Gershwin; jazz in a high hat; jazz that had conquered the establishment and made it swing.

Gershwin played piano. You couldn't get the same effect with a guitar if only. Her fingers began to tingle, the energy spreading up to her shoulders, blocking out everything. Rhapsody in Blue; she knew the music. She had the technical knowledge. She had the magic that could put it all together.

"Give me the stage," she said suddenly.

"What?"

"Stand aside and let me have the piano."

"All right, Princess. I hope you know what you're doing."

The others stood back as Adam Smith motioned them out of the way, giving Zoe center stage. If Zoe had been aware of the audience, she would have seen them puzzled, yet charitably receptive. No doubt they were expecting a competently rendered classic.

What they got was Gershwin. Notes penned light years away. Notes that gripped their souls in a velvet vice. When she was done they gave her an ovation that would have satisfied the most demanding diva. Kendel led her away from the piano like a reigning queen.

"I thought you only played guitar," he said.

"I do."

"Oh, I see, and what was that?"

"I knew the music backwards. It's my favorite piece by a man named Gershwin. I just willed myself to know how to play it on the piano. You can't play that stuff on a guitar and get the proper effect. In fact, for the real sound, you need a whole orchestra."

Kendel chuckled softly.

"An orchestra playing jazz?"

"Yes, an orchestra. Jazz won't stay in speakeasies and bordellos forever. I guess I just wanted to show them that."

From the direction of the band the quiet strains of a slow romantic tune invaded their awareness. Kendel's right arm encircled Zoe's waist and he began to lead her around the dance floor. Around them conversation returned to normal and the party continued.

"Where do you come from?" Kendel asked.

"Earth," said Zoe.

"Got any proof?"

"Not much."

"Going back soon?"

"Don't know."

"How do I convince you to stay?"

Kendel was serious now, serious enough to put a lump in Zoe's throat and a tremble in her voice.

"Believe me."

Kendel stopped dancing and pulled Zoe close. Belief in anything but the power of a man and a woman together became irrelevant. They kissed softly at first, then again as deeply as the presence of onlookers would allow.

Along the outside wall of the long, wide music room were three sets of French doors that opened out into the garden. The night was quite cool, so in spite of the press of bodies on the dance floor, the glass doors had remained closed. The shattering concussion of an explosion opened the center doors, sending a shower of glass everywhere.

By the time the smoke and confusion had cleared, twelve heavily armed masked men lined the walls of the room! They did nothing. They said nothing. When all was still and silent a thirteenth masked man appeared out of the gloom of the darkened garden.

This last man was unarmed, but he did not come unencumbered. He was dragging the broken body of a man by the collar of his jacket, moving him along as easily as one might take out the garbage.

The man groaned incoherently as he was dumped on the dance floor, showing that no matter what he looked like, he was still alive. Kendel fell to his knees beside the battered body.

"Len! Tolino I'll see you fry so help me."

The battered man struggled to speak.

"Boss. . .get out."

Overwhelmed by the fall from heady romance into nightmarish horror, Zoe simply stood where Kendel had left her. She tried desperately to think, to dredge up some action that would defend this room full of innocent people from this surreal invasion. Before she could pull any useful thought from her fear-frozen brain, a damp pad clamped over her nose. A fleeting attempt at a struggle was all she could manage before the ether shut down her system and her mind took a much needed rest.

CHAPTER 28

"Zoe!"

Someone was yelling Zoe wished they would stop. She felt as if her head had been stuffed full of cotton wool mixed liberally with bits of broken glass. It was a condition that did not mix well with noise.

"Zoe!"

There was that voice again, a nice warm familiar voice. The voice was the only thing that was warm. Everything else was November cold.

"Can't we go home now, Mom. I hate skating."

No that didn't belong. It was a memory, just an old memory.

"Zoe Darby wake up!"

"Zoe Crane, my name's Zoe Crane."

"That's just dandy. Well, it's going to be Zoe Darby on your tombstone if there's anything left to bury."

Zoe forced her eyes open with a snap and came face to face with what looked very much like a dead pig. Considering the fact she was trying to fight her way back to reality this odd vision wasn't helping.

"Kendel?" she asked.

"Yes."

His voice sounded relieved that she was finally answering and frustrated at the same time.

"Pardon me for wasting time with minutiae, but is this a dead pig?" she asked.

"Yes, Zoe. That is a dead pig."

"Yuk!"

Zoe pushed her attention beyond that of the porcine face hanging six inches from her nose and found that, not only was she sitting on a cold cement floor, but her hands had been pulled behind her and tied firmly to a metal post. A little careful sliding of the ropes up the post brought her to a standing position, and thus gave her an entirely different prospective on the world.

It was a small, cold world, hung with hooks attached to a rack, which was in turn bolted to the ceiling. Most of the hooks held some manner of animal carcass. One, on the far side of the little room, held Joshua Kendel.

"You look awful," she said. "Are you hurt?"

Kendel's face was very pale. His lips were touched with blue. His wrists had been tied together, then looped over the hook above him and although his feet could reach the ground he seemed to sag so that his arms held much of his weight.

"My right leg hurts like hell. I think a bone is broken. I know it's at least cracked."

"Okay. Stupid question number three. Where are we?"

"Waterfront meat packing plant, I think. We rode here in the trunk of a car. That's when my leg got it, they slammed the trunk lid before I was in all the way. Too impatient to get here and start the fun, I guess."

"I'm sorry, Joshua. I should have done something back at the house. But when it happened all I could think of was how afraid I was."

"Zoe, it takes a lot of training for a person to act even though they're terrified. It's not your fault."

"Was anyone killed?"

For a moment Kendel had to struggle to contain his emotions.

"Not that I could see. The man you saw who was hurt was Detective Len Barker. He's connected with my office and in charge of my protection. He's a good friend. When they dragged me away from him he was still breathing. It was Malone who led the raid. I'd know that bulk anywhere."

"What about Tolino?"

"Tolino would have been somewhere else, somewhere very public. We were stuffed in here until Tolino can visit personally."

Zoe began to shiver slightly. She told herself firmly it was because of the cold. She couldn't afford to be frightened. She'd allowed herself to give into her fear at the house and that had brought them here.

"Nothing like a nice dose of hypothermia to make a guest feel wanted. I think it's time we left."

Zoe began to examine the ropes that bound her to the post. The knots were far too tight for her numb fingers to try to untie. They would have to be cut.

A vision began in her mind of a small round spinning blade cutting into a multi-colored cast. She had fallen off her bicycle and broken her arm, thus becoming an instant celebrity. Everyone in her kindergarten class had drawn something on the cast. The principal had even come into the class and signed his name for luck. Then there was the trip to the hospital to have the cast cut off.

The vivid memory of that common childhood adventure blurred into the present day horror. The memory became real. A small round metal blade cutting into a plaster cast began fraying particles of hemp. The rope broke apart so suddenly that Zoe fell forward, escaping sudden contact with the cement floor only by grabbing the carcass of the pig hanging in front of her.

"Sorry, little piggy, but that's what you get for going to market instead of going home like a good boy."

Zoe patted the swine on its cold empty head and began to weave her way through the room toward Kendel.

"You did it again," said Kendel.

"Did what again?"

"That trick, whatever it is you do, you did it. I'd almost convinced myself that it was just my imagination."

Zoe shook her head.

"Denial is not a healthy thing, Joshua. In this case it could get us both dead."

Zoe gripped his forearms firmly to hold him steady as she again dredged up the vivid memory of the small spinning blade. This time Kendel was able to see what was happening. His fascination with the sight of the ropes being severed by the invisible force was so complete that when the ropes no longer held him up he almost fell into Zoe's arms.

Supporting him as well as she could Zoe wrapped his left arm around her shoulders. She helped him to the door of the walk-in cooler, saying,

"Let's go, Hop-a-long. We have to get out of here."

"I'm going to kill that Malone," Kendel muttered between clenched teeth.

"That's it! You keep thinking nice warm thoughts. I'm going to get this door open."

"There's bound to be a guard," said Kendel.

"I know."

Zoe studied the door and a confused panic began to blur her confidence. On the inside it was a blank sheet of metal, innocent of a latch of any kind. She had no memory of being on the outside.

"Well?" said Kendel expectantly.

"I don't know how to open it. I don't think I've ever been in a regular butcher shop. I've certainly never been in a meat packing plant. I don't even know what the latch on the outside of a door like this looks like."

Panic, fear and discomfort began to do a dance in Zoe's head. There was no way it was going to end like this. It couldn't.

"How did you buy your meat?" Kendel asked.

"Pre-packaged, in Styrofoam trays wrapped in cellophane."

Kendel stared at her as if she were speaking Latin.

"What the hell is cellophane?" he asked.

"Petroleum based polymer?" Zoe said limply.

"Sorry I asked. We have to get out of here Zoe. How do we open the door?" he said in exasperation. "Knock?"

Zoe looked at the pale man leaning against the freezer wall and felt the unfocused panic that had filled her change. There was better use for that energy. If you couldn't open a door quietly, then the only alternative was to open it any way you could.

"Yes. That is exactly what we do. We knock."

The fear in her voice was gone. She stood as far back from the door as the well-packed freezer would allow.

"Bang on the door as hard as you can, then get out of the way."

Kendel did as he was told, filling the metal room with the sound of three echoing thumps. As he hopped out of the line of fire, he crouched behind a pile of boxes.

139

"You'll get out soon enough, Kendel. Then you'll wish you were back in!"

The words were muffled by the thick insulated door. The prisoners heard and understood them all the same. The harsh sarcastic laughter that followed could not have been clearer.

Zoe smiled grimly at the sound. It made what she had to do a lot easier. She closed her eyes and in her mind saw a huge clenched fist. It reared back and hit the door hard!

When Kendel looked out from behind the boxes he had ducked behind the door was not simply open it was gone! Limping toward the open portal he saw that it was not really gone. It had simply been pushed off its hinges as if by a huge invisible hand, then slammed against the floor. Of course it wasn't actually flat against the floor.

"You got him!"

Zoe went to Kendel's side and looped his right arm around her shoulder. Reluctantly he let her carry some of his weight.

"Ya, I guess I did. Come on let's go!"

As they stepped around the tilted metal rectangle a rivulet of blood began to inch its way out from under a place near the top. In spite of herself, Zoe stopped and bent slightly as if to peek under the macabre blanket.

Kendel stopped her with a firm hand on her shoulder that had nothing to do with his support.

"Don't look. I've seen stuff like that. Believe me, it's not pretty."

"Inefficacy is never pretty, Mr. Kendel."

It was Tolino.

CHAPTER 29

The gangster leader stood in the open door beside one of six loading docks lining the wall to the right of the freezer. He entered the big high-ceilinged building and was immediately joined by six tall, squarely-built men. Their spectacular escape had done them no good at all.

"This is the second time a representative of mine has been inefficient in his dealings with you, Kendel. Good help is so hard to find."

"They were searched, Mr. Tolino. I did it myself," said Malone.

Malone stood behind them in the open doorway. Following the others in, he took his place standing at Tolino's right. The gangster stared at Zoe, his discomfort at her appearance now completely apparent.

"You searched the girl?" Tolino asked.

"She was out cold. Who'd know she'd wake up before we got back? Anyway what's a girl like that gonna carry that would break a door down?"

Zoe favored the confused man with a thin smile and mouthed the words, "I know." Malone started at this silent revelation and appeared not to hear when his boss spoke again.

"You are getting down right careless, Malone. We are going to have to have a talk."

Tolino strolled across the floor to examine the collapsed door.

Not even a scorch mark. If you weren't so rich already, Kendel, you could go into safe-blowing and clean up."

Kendel said, "Tolino, the only thing I want to 'clean up' is you."

Tolino favored his guest with a wide viper's smile.

"Very poetic. You should be in the opera. I'll tell you what, Mr. Kendel. We're business men you and I. I'll give you a proposition. You return the ledgers you stole from me and I'll let you and your woman go."

Kendel shook his head slowly.

"I can't do that, Tolino; not even for Zoe's sake. A representative from the Federal Bureau met with my people this afternoon. They confiscated everything. They're going to put their experts on that stuff and when they're finished you will get sent up for income-tax evasion."

Tolino stared at his captives with open-mouthed astonishment. He turned to Malone, who at that moment was dealing with problems of his own. Staring around at some invisible horror, Malone began stepping gradually away from his companions. For some unknown reason the man's nervous system seemed to be completely unraveling.

"You're dead!" he gasped.

"Malone, what the hell?" asked Tolino wonderingly.

"You're all dead!"

"What's happening here?" Kendel whispered to Zoe.

Zoe's eyes were far off and vague. Her lips drawn up in a crooked smile. When she spoke she sounded like a sleep walker.

"He's seeing his victims. All of them. The moment one pops into his head, that person also appears like a half-solid shadow. You should see it, Kendel. This man has killed an awful lot of people. It's like NIGHT OF THE LIVING DEAD, with Melinda in the lead. He's not going to be able to take much more."

"I'll finish this. I'll finish you all. I did it once. I'll do it again!"

Malone was yelling now. Grabbing for the place under his coat where he kept his note pad. Only this time, instead of the pad, he produced a large automatic weapon. An explosion brought Zoe out of her trance with a jerk, sending the shadowy legion of Malone's victims back to the void from which they came.

One of Tolino's men held a gun. A second was kneeling by Malone's still body. This second man looked up and shook his head.

"I'm sorry, boss," said the man with the gun. "He was going crazy."

"You did right, Vito. Don't worry," said Tolino. "I would have done it myself. You just moved a little faster. Leave him there. We'll do right by him as soon as we take care of business."

Angry now as if he had been forced to do something against his will and sensed that somehow they were responsible Tolino studied Zoe and Kendel for a long minute. Still supporting the injured Kendel, Zoe stared back.

She felt worn down empty. The effort of cutting the ropes, then opening the freezer, and finally inducing Malone's suicidal madness, had drained her to the point that when her eyes met Tolino's, it took every ounce of spirit she had to simply stare him down. All she could feel was fear.

"Our last little meeting should have happened here," Tolino began. "Unfortunately they were unloading a late shipment that night and the place was full of honest working men. I like honest working men. They're some of my best customers. Follow me."

Not wanting the sort of help their well-muscled escorts were prepared to provide. Kendel and Zoe struggled to keep up with Tolino as he strolled past a row of large machines that had something to do with processing the meat kept in the cold rooms lining two walls of the large building.

Tolino paused in front of one. It was an ancient looking machine appearing to be nothing more than a huge boiler connected with pipes to a large covered vat.

"I couldn't tell you what the rest of these things do," Tolino said as he adjusted several dials on the boiler and checked what looked like a pilot light.

"However, I have found this one very useful. They take any animals that you can't eat say the meat's gone bad, and they put them in here along with the parts of the animals that you don't eat anyway. Then they boil the stuff down until they can drain off the fat for make-up and other stuff like that. After that they take what's left, grind it up, and make it into feed for pigs. That's what I'm gonna do with you."

Tolino's short explanation had all the qualities of a well-rehearsed, oft delivered speech. While this was happening, one of the men climbed the short ladder attached to the vat and opened a large hatch in its side. After climbing down the ladder he slyly slipped the huge wad of gum in his mouth out and onto the inner side of the ladder just where they would have to grip it to climb up.

Zoe's mind registered the sick practical joke with the same numb realization that the emotions within her no longer had the power to affect matter.

143

Malone was dead. Her reason for being here was gone. The only problem was, she was still here!

Clearly enjoying his self-indulgent build-up to their murder, Nick Tolino droned on.

"The rendering vat is empty right now. Once the water in the boiler reaches the correct temperature, it is automatically dumped into the vat."

Tolino tapped the gauge that would register the temperature and then operate the switch that would send the gallons of boiling water into the vat. It was mechanical, not electronic. Of course it was mechanical! This was nineteen-twenty-nine!

Zoe stepped out from under Kendel's arm. Pausing in front of the ladder, she looked at where the men were standing, making it seem as if she were taking one last look at the world. She reached out with one hand and lightly gripped the ladder. With one finger she scooped the gum off the rusted metal.

When she made her break, she did in the form of a bank shot, bouncing off the boiler workings directly beside Tolino, then ricocheting between two of his stunned men. The meek sacrificial lamb had turned gazelle!

"Run, Zoe! Don't look back! RUN!"

Kendel's yell of encouragement ended in a single gunshot, the fading echoes of which were punctuated by a prolonged cry of agony. Zoe cringed at the sound of his pain, knowing at the same time that he had been right. She had to get out of there and looking back was the last thing on her mind!

Covering the distance they had just walked in an instant, Zoe skidded to a stop a heartbeat long, then took off along the row of meat lockers. The open door, which the gangsters had used to enter the building was being guarded by a surprised looking man holding a machine-gun. The odds of getting away were shrinking fast!

CHAPTER 30

Terror gripped Zoe's throat. Her breath came in harsh gasps. Panic prompted tears turned the already dimly lit building into a blurred nightmare of ominous machinery set to the music of pounding feet.

There was no way this was going to work, not this part anyway. Unfortunately, the only way she would find out if the rest succeeded would be when everything else failed.

A huge male figure loomed up out of the darkness. Pre-programmed by a lifetime of television combined with a fondness for action-adventure films, Zoe kicked out at the obstruction. The man dropped to the ground, bent double at the groin.

It flashed through Zoe's mind that she should grab the man's gun. An instant later, it was too late. The weapon had dropped and slid away under a machine and the hood's not too distant companions were closing the painfully small gap between them with stunning swiftness. With a half-crawling roll she dove under a long sheltering conveyor belt near the wall.

Set in the wall was the tantalizing vision of a door. Not knowing whether it was safe or not, but afraid of being caught where she was, Zoe made a break for the exit.

She turned the doorknob and leaned hard. The night air was early-dawn cool. A cloudless sky stretched out displaying an unending canopy of stars. One star was her star. Her sun, life-giving light for the planet that was home.

Without warning, a lightning flash of pain exploded in her head. She fell and was lifted up then thrown over a shoulder. Her awareness did not fade, yet her strength to do anything about what she saw and felt had been burned away with the throbbing fire that had settled into her brain.

"Will you hurry up! She has to be in there when the dump happens for it to work properly."

Darkness replaced the light of the warehouse. She fell hard onto a smooth metal surface. Seemingly miles above her, the rectangle of light that was the door to freedom and life disappeared with an echoing crash that had in it all the certainty of death.

The interior of the huge rendering cauldron was perfectly black. Within this artificial midnight a trembling hand reached out. Zoe grasped the hand and held it tightly. It was all she could do.

Every time she moved a wave of nausea hit that threatened to turn her stomach inside out. This was no detective show hit on the head where the hero takes a short nap for about as long as it takes to run a few commercials. This was pain with a capital P that begged for an ambulance, a doctor, and a nice soft bed.

"Joshua?"

Kendel's breath was labored. When he spoke it was clear he was coping with a massive amount of pain.

"Damn sadist shot my good leg. He didn't want me dead. He likes to hear the screams when the boiler dumps the water into the vat."

"I wish. I wish I could do something."

"Why can't you? What happened? From the moment Malone got it, it was like you were the one who turned ghost."

Zoe felt salt water on her cheeks and knew she was crying.

"I can't do it anymore. The power died along with Malone."

"Then we really are dead," Kendel said.

"Not necessarily."

Zoe, tried to sound confident in spite of the sob in her voice.

"Did you notice that boiler. It's incredibly old. I bet it's unsafe at high temperatures. If something were to gum up the temperature gauge that trips the dump switch, it would likely just sit there getting hotter and hotter. There might even be an explosion."

"What are you saying?" Kendel asked.

Zoe had no chance to explain. The boiling vat began to vibrate, shaking the entire structure and sending waves of agony through her head and down into her whole nervous system. A splash of boiling water squirted out of the pipe that came from the boiler. It landed on her legs.

The scream she heard was hers and yet it sounded as if it came from a long way off. Her broken head protested yet again and finally took charge, sending her to that dark quiet place where pain has no power and terror cannot go.

*****

Soft strong hands and thick warm blankets, the hands offered cool fresh water in a kind of mug with a porcelain spout. Zoe drank without lifting her head from the pillow, without opening her eyes. She knew these blankets, this bed. They told her that she would be safe and even her most basic needs would be anticipated.

This was her bed in Joshua Kendel's mansion home. She was safe, and just for the moment she felt selfish enough to want to avoid having to ask where Kendel was; or if he was even alive.

*****

It was almost two weeks before the doctor aided and abetted by a hovering Aunt Minny would let Zoe make the trip to the hospital to see Kendel. They were two weeks full of rest, quiet, and education. Much of the time was spent deep in thought.

She thought about hard decisions, about love and most of all about belonging. From belonging it was only a short mental step to think about Miss Emily, the old woman who had come from somewhere else and stayed. She had stayed yet Zoe suspected that never once had she felt like she belonged.

Once at the hospital, Kendel's doctor explained what his condition was in carefully-phrased terms. Zoe didn't ask questions. By now she knew any hard truth would be either avoided, or sugar-coated to the point of almost total unreality.

Zoe walked into the room alone. Kendel's legs were in traction. An operation had been necessary to try to put them into at least a semblance of good form. In preparation for her visit, the head of his bed had been cranked up to a forty-five degree angle.

"God, it's good to see you!"

His eyes were clouded with the shadow of pain held in check with drugs, but his smile was warm and alive. She went and stood beside the bed.

"I wanted to come before this, but your Aunt and the doctor have been treating me like a porcelain egg. To be honest, at first I felt the part. It's been kind of an interesting experience, but given time even kid-gloves can start to chafe."

He took her hand and held it tight, his pale face looking up at hers. Zoe felt from him a warmth that was almost frightening in its strength. It was a warmth that would force her to make a decision about the future, one way, or the other.

He said, "I never want you to be hurt again; not even by the truth. I want to take care of you."

"Then tell me the truth. What happened at the warehouse?"

Kendel looked down at his legs. He closed his eyes for a moment and licked his lips as if trying to search for just the right words. Words that would tell the truth yet hide at least some of the grisly reality involved.

"Something must have gone wrong with the temperature gauge. The boiler exploded. Tolino and his men were."

Kendel paused as if he were unsure of how to continue.

"Par-boiled?" Zoe suggested, flippantly.

"Killed instantly," Kendel said flatly.

"What about...."

Zoe nodded her head toward Kendel's legs.

"I don't remember it myself and it's probably just as well. The cauldron we were in was pushed over by the explosion and rolled about fifty feet. What with the break and the bullet and the extra damage done by all that bouncing around, I'm lucky they didn't have to amputate.

The doctor put them back together as best he could. The rest is up to mother nature. In about three months I should be able to try walking. I might need braces; for how long they don't know."

"Do they know what gummed up the temperature gauge?" Zoe asked.

"No. Their best guess is rust. The thing was so old it was almost a museum piece."

"The hot water must have washed it all away."

Kendel stared back blankly. It was an almost comical expression that had Zoe stifling a fit of giggles before they got out of control.

"One of Tolino's men stuck a big wad of chewing gum on the ladder leading into the vat. One of us was supposed to get a gummed up hand when we climbed into the vat. When I watched him step away from the ladder I noticed the temperature gauge for the boiler. I'm not sure if I thought the whole thing through completely. All I remember is thinking that if I gummed up the gauge then the boiler might overheat and explode."

Kendel shook his head in disbelief.

"I have never met a woman who thought the way you do. You're incredible."

"No, I'm not. What I am, is the product of over sixty years of social evolution. I've had a pretty conservative upbringing, but even so I couldn't think the way a woman of this time thinks if I tried. I'm used to walking through open doors, not peering through windows."

"Still on about that, are you?" Kendel said, indulgently.

He couldn't believe. He may have believed in the heat of action, but in the naked light of day it was simply not possible. A feeling that was equal parts frustration and sadness put a lump in Zoe's throat and a tightness in her chest. She took a deep breath and let it out slowly in an attempt to keep her mood light.

"I can't avoid it. It's the truth." Her voice was deadly serious in spite of her efforts. "I'm not from here; not from this time, and not from this planet."

He countered her seriousness with a romantic lightness.

"You're not thinking of going now, are you? I had some plans for us."

"I haven't seen any of the lights Miss Emily talked about. I think one thing has been holding me back. It's a little thing on the face of it, but in time it could grow to mean a lot."

"I love you."

There it was. It was out in the open and it had to be faced. He was a romance-novel hero, handsome, intelligent, rich. She'd be a fool to turn him down, except . . .

"I know you love me, but do you believe me?" she asked.

"I've tried Zoe, but..."

Kendel opened his mouth but the explanation would not come. Zoe saw that it would likely never come.

She felt something very close to love for this man. Only her preoccupation with her mission had interrupted that process. Before that thing called "falling in love" could be allowed to happen an important choice would have to be made.

The choice involved a question. How important was belief? How long could she continue to live happily in a place where not even the one she held dear believed in her past? Pulling her hand from his, she crossed her arms, holding them tightly against her body, embracing her disappointment.

As she searched for the right words to say, her eyes followed the clamps and pulleys that held his legs taunt. In her mind's eye, she saw the face of Miss Emily, satisfied with her choice; yet lonely. It had been the loneliness of the outsider who is never completely believed. Not even by the ones who loved and cared for her. Loved but alone would Emily have stayed if there had been anything to pull her back?

"When are you going to start working again?" she asked, filling the void their conflict had created.

"I quit. My term was almost over and it didn't seem right to hang onto the office simply for the sake of the name. It'll take me a quite a while to get back on my feet again, if I ever do. After that, I'm not sure. I think I'm ready to do something different."

"What about politics?" Zoe asked.

"Zoe, I might never walk on my own again. I don't have much of a choice so I guess I'll have to get used to the idea."

"It's better than being dead," Zoe said.

"A lot better but it still leaves me with a problem. Who'd vote for a crippled politician?"

"Oh, I don't know. If you use the newspapers and radio properly, then the people will connect you with what you say, not what you look like. What's more important a great body or a great mind? I can imagine a president in braces, a marine on either side to help him along."

"You have a big imagination," said Kendel.

"It happened. His name was Roosevelt. He had polio, but that didn't stop him from being one of the greatest presidents his country ever had. He died years before I was born."

"That again."

Kendel lay his head back in the pillow and closed his eyes as if the short visit had tired him more than he wanted to admit. Zoe knew that it was more than physical fatigue. He wanted her to tell him that it was all a game.

The watch she had showed him was just a trick. She was an orphan out to seek her fortune. A love child hiding from the disgrace of her past.

It was impossible. Even Miss Emily with her sad shadow past had shared the truth about what she was with her adopted family. That family had in turn at least pretended to believe. Roots could not be denied, no matter how shallow.

Zoe turned away from the bed, her eyes wandering aimlessly about the room. Eventually she looked up.

A round light fixture hung from a chain attached to the ceiling. Because of the bright sun streaming through the window, the light was not turned on. The moment Zoe looked up, something began in the center of the hanging globe, a sparkling twinkle that grew until there was no doubt what was happening.

"I'm sorry, Joshua. If I stayed very much longer, I know I'd start to love you. It would be so easy to just let it happen. The problem is I have roots elsewhere; roots you don't even believe exist. Those roots have never had a chance to grow. I think I'd like to see what would happen if I gave them that chance."

The light grew bright, then blinding. Zoe stretched her hands up toward the beckoning torch and reality around her became a brightly blurred canvas of color without shape, fire without heat.

She traveled without fear at a speed beyond time. She had gone else-where and had learned, in the space of days, more than she had ever thought possible. It was time to give home another chance.

CHAPTER 31

Muted music filled the room. Yolanda Wren rolled over in bed and looked at the clock radio. It wasn't due to go off for another twenty minutes.

Numbly, she realized what had gotten her up ahead of time. The curio cabinet across from the door seemed to almost vibrate with sound. Mixed in with the oddly realistic toys and small statuary were music boxes. Some had moving parts. Others were still, letting the music stand on its own.

Something in this early-morning hour had turned them on, all of them. The sound created a strange tangled echoing web of sensation that filled the room. Trembling slightly, Yolanda Wren sat on the end of her bed and watched as a tiny ballerina, set at the front of one shelf, spun around on her little stage.

For three days and three nights, the Shadow Man had stayed by the street lamp, slept in his doorway. Whenever she had looked his way he had smiled his dry mummy's smile, planting his seeds of doubt.

She tried not to hate him for being right. As keeper of the crystal, it was her power that directed travelers and then brought them home. An undirected traveler had only the slimmest chance of returning alone.

There was only one other chance. A chance the Shadow Man would never understand. Hope and renewal were things he knew of only from their absence.

Suddenly that invisible power that had started the clashing tangle of sound vanished. The ballerina stopped in mid-pirouette. But the room was not silent.

Something was coming, breaking the air with a high piercing whine. Moving at the speed of dreams it vibrated the cabinet; threatening to break it apart!

Yolanda Wren jumped from her bed. She had time only to unlatch the cabinet doors and open them wide before a force strong enough to bend space and time to its will pushed her aside, knocking her off her feet!

Zoe grabbed a bedpost, pulled herself to a sitting position and looked up at the simple crystal ball sitting on its silver ring. A black velvet cloth hung off the shelf. Slowly it slipped and fell to the floor.

Yolanda Wren leaned forward and picked up the scrap. She was on the floor to the right of the cabinet, pajama-clad legs splayed wide in front of her. To Zoe, she presented an incongruous picture, as if she had been tossed aside by the rudest of bullies and didn't know what to do next.

What she did next was smile a soft morning smile, blush, then, wonder of wonders, she actually giggled. The effect was startling. The mysterious wise woman had become a middle-aged maiden aunt caught by a childish practical joke and ready to play the good sport. Yet, underneath it all, the wise woman was still there.

"Now you know how the glass was broken."

Zoe looked back up at the ball.

"You fell though it from the inside?"

"I'm the only one who ever has until now. Now that you have too, we have a lot to talk about. I wasn't sure before. It made the waiting hard."

Yolanda Wren climbed to her feet draped the cloth over the ball and closed the cupboard doors. She then donned her robe.

Zoe also got to her feet, realizing at the same time that she was wearing the same clothes in which she had started her journey. Wordless she followed her hostess into the kitchen. The place where the whole adventure had started.

"I shall make Darjeeling tea this time. We need to wake up. I certainly do at any rate. You caught me off guard. This has never happened before. Not to me, at least."

Once again Zoe sat in the chair by the door.

"What has never happened before?"

"You traveled on your own," said Yolanda.

The words held some importance beyond Zoe's understanding. As if trying to create time in which to solve a difficult problem, Yolanda Wren turned the fire on under the kettle, then pulled a plate of muffins out of a bread box and put them on the table along with a container of margarine.

This done, she put out the same mugs they had used in their early morning meeting and put the tea pot on the table next to a box of bags.

Preparations complete, she sat waiting for the kettle to boil.

"Other than myself and the woman who passed the ball on to me, no one I know has ever been able to travel and return unaided. I wasn't sure anyone would ever be able to go at all. Oh she did tell me it would happen someday, but it's been a very long time."

"How does it usually happen?" Zoe asked. "They do come back, don't they?"

"Most do. A few have nothing to return to; they make a better life else-where. It all depends. Generally I get an image in my mind of the traveler wanting to come home. When that happens I take the ball out, put it on the table and will them to return. Not as convenient as ruby slippers, but I seldom get any complaints."

Slowly, Zoe's mind began to add up what Yolanda was saying and come to some conclusions.

"Those toys, they have something to do with this, don't they?"

"Some were passed along by my mentor who had gathered them during her apprenticeship. Quite a few I brought back myself from during my time of learning. Some were given to me by travelers. They claim to have profited by their travels but could not face owning a reminder of their lessons. I keep the tokens as proof that even miracles can fail to teach a mind that will not learn."

"How long have I been gone?"

"Three days and three nights, give or take a few hours. Quite Biblical, when you come to think of it. Did you learn what you needed to know?"

"I think so. I learned about fear, and being alone, and being myself. Not a bad start to a new life."

"Not bad at all."

The kettle began to steam. Yolanda rose and filled the teapot with hot water.

"What do you want to do next?" she asked.

Zoe leaned back, resting her head against the wall and stretching her legs out in front of her. She closed her eyes for a moment to think. Her joy in making music, reawakened by her brief glimpse of professional life, was one possible career path.

Yet even with her talent it could take a long time to achieve professional accreditation. Meanwhile, the bills would insist on being paid. She also wanted to finish high school and continue on to a university. This meant she would have to have a job.

Stimulated by the powerful question of what to do, a window in her mind opened and knowledge flooded in, almost blinding her with its power. The knowledge came in the form of a tableau. Her mother, confused, distraught, sat in a chair in the living room. Her father, with the look of a man who has lost more than he knew he had, stood looking out their front window.

Zoe opened her eyes. For a moment the vivid mental picture hung around her like a hologram, then it was gone.

"You had a vision just now, didn't you?"

Zoe looked over to find Yolanda Wren pouring tea. The woman's eyes were filled with a kind of wistful understanding that was as much memory as it was knowledge. She set the teapot down and sat waiting for Zoe to speak.

"How did you know?" Zoe asked.

"I had my first vision just after my first voyage. After my second, I was able to read the cards. After the third, I began to use the crystal to see the future. That was how my mentor knew that it was I she was meant to pass the crystal on to. The most important sign was the ability to travel without direction. The talents were simply icing on the cake."

"WELCOME APPRENTICE! THE SHADOW MAN WELCOMES YOU TO THE BATTLE OF HOPE AND DESPAIR!"

Zoe gripped her head. The words had resounded in her mind like a mental assault.

"Oh God what was that!" Zoe gasped.

Yolanda Wren sipped her tea. It was clear she had heard the frightening greeting but instead of frightened she seemed victorious.

"That was the Shadow Man. He is the darkness against which the crystal fights. He's spent the last three days telling me that I'd lost you and you were going to spend the rest of your life trapped on some strange world whether you wanted to be there or not."

Zoe remembered her arriving at this haven and said;

"The bum in the street."

"That was him. He is no danger to us directly. He exists to try and push away people who are drawn to the crystal. "

Yolanda frowned slightly.

"Actually I should say he is no danger to me. You must try very hard to withstand his influence. He will try and drive you away. If he does, then when I die the line of crystal keepers will end and a window of hope will be closed forever. Remember this Zoe. Despair is not fatal, it's what it causes you to do that is the danger."

Zoe took her tea and sipped.

"I feel like I've been drafted."

Yolanda chuckled softly.

"I don't blame you. I felt a bit like that myself."

"Does this mean I now have to become a fortune teller?" asked Zoe.

"Not at all. My mentor was a physician. However, I'd hazard a guess she healed more people with her inner power than she ever did with drugs. She was the Keeper of the Crystal, as I am, as you will be."

"As I will be," echoed Zoe.

"Tell me your vision," Yolanda prompted.

"I saw my parents. They're worried. It's funny, I get the feeling that if I went back things would be different."

"Things will. It won't be easy. It's very hard for adults who are set in their ways to change, but they can. I think you should go back finish growing up. I'm not ready to pass the ball on yet, and in spite of what you have learned, you are far from ready to receive it."

"What will I tell them when they ask where I've been? I have to tell them something," wondered Zoe.

"Tell them you've been on a religious retreat. That will leave the door open for future 'retreats'. You'll know when it's time to go again. Your feet will begin to move. Aimless at first, you will soon find yourself in my garden, then in my reading room. Then you will remove the cover from the ball and say 'Crystal, take me elsewhere.'."

"Then someday the crystal will belong to me."

"Yes it will. One day in the future, when I am very old and sick, I will give all I own to you and then I will say those words for the last time. I wonder where I'll go?"

Zoe thought of this picture for a long moment and found that she liked it a great deal.

"Can I come even if I don't need to go somewhere?"

The woman sitting across from her smiled.

"I could hardly think of myself as your mentor if I only saw you once or twice a year, now could I?" Yolanda chided. "You need instruction. My first instruction to you is to go to my living room and phone home."

Zoe walked down the long, narrow hall and into the living room. She found the telephone on an end table next to the couch she had not had a chance to sleep on.

Feeling a pull her eyes went from the couch to the room's view of the street. The man from her arrival stood looking up at the window. His eyes were hidden by his ragged hair but she felt them just the same. He bowed a strange courtly bow. Standing he backed away his solid figure crumbling and blowing away like dust until he was gone. Zoe wasn't afraid. She had an idea she might be in the future but for now she had no room for fear.

She reached for the phone but before dialing, she was distracted by a strange lump in the smoothness of her back pocket. She slipped her hand into the space, more of a decorative patch than pocket, and pulled out a small silver charm hanging on a bracelet-sized chain.

It was a guitar. Zoe stared in wonder. It was an exquisitely detailed duplicate of the instrument she had played on that far-off planet.

Sitting in the palm of her hand, its miniature surfaces reflected the morning light like fire. In unconscious echo of the woman who sat in the apartment's kitchen drinking tea, the corners of Zoe's mouth drew up in a small secret smile.

She picked up the phone. Gripping the little charm tightly, she dialed her home number, wondering all the while what the next charm might be.

www.ingramcontent.com/pod-product-compliance
Lightning Source LLC
Chambersburg PA
CBHW050751250626
47155CB00005B/2010